Running Wild

The Loves of Lakeside

Running Wild

MIMI FRANCIS

4 Horsemen
Publications, Inc.

Published By: 4 Horsemen Publications, Inc.

4 Horsemen Publications, Inc.
PO Box 417
Sylva, NC 28779
4horsemenpublications.com
info@4horsemenpublications.com

Cover &Typesetting by Autumn Skye
Edited by Kris Cotter

Library of Congress Control Number: 2025948018

Paperback ISBN-13: 979-8-8232-1007-2

Dedication

Thank you to the people of Lakeside, Montana, for letting me manipulate your little town to fit my stories. Visiting Lakeside is like coming home.

Table of Contents

Chapter 1

Teddie

*T*heodora "Teddie" Calloway shoved herself away from her desk and stretched. She hated the days she was stuck inside ordering supplies and running numbers. She preferred being outside working on the ranch, riding her horse, or helping with the cattle or the cherry harvest.

Teddie checked her watch. It was almost five, and she still had to talk to Wyatt about moving the cattle and check with Luke about the hay sales. Her day rarely ended at sunset.

Helping run one of the largest ranches in Lakeside, Montana wasn't an easy feat, especially as a woman and the daughter of a former military man. Fortunately, she was up to the task. In fact, she had been the one to get Cherry Ridge Ranch running in the black for the first time since her father took over thirty years ago, and she'd kept it there for almost four years. If the Colonel listened to her ideas, they might turn their small family fortune into an enormous family fortune.

Teddie looked out the large, glass window overlooking the cherry orchard and the barn. She loved the view, but she loved being outside even more, so she shut her computer down, grabbed her hat, and made her way outside, walking down the path along the side of the house and past the orchard. After she moved back to the ranch to work for Cherry Ridge, her father had the guesthouse behind the main house converted into an office space. Two of the bedrooms and the main living area now served as offices, and the last bedroom had become a storage room lined with filing cabinets. It was where she spent most of her days.

She was almost to the barn when she heard her father yelling, so she slipped behind a tree to listen.

Her father, Colonel Everett Calloway, appeared to be involved in a heated discussion with Cherry Ridge's foreman, Wyatt Dawson. The Colonel's arms gesticulated wildly, and his shouting occasionally reached her ears. Wyatt stood with his arms crossed and his lips drawn together, the only outward sign of his irritation. Dark glasses covered his eyes, but Teddie was sure if she saw them, his steel-blue orbs would be flashing in anger.

"Take care of it, Dawson," her father shouted before spinning on his custom-made cowboy boots and stalking across the manicured lawn toward the kitchen entrance. Teddie watched him go, wondering what ridiculous thing he'd demanded of his staff this time.

Intent on talking to Wyatt—and hopefully smoothing things over—she continued walking to the barn. She was almost there when a horn honked behind her. Turning, she saw her mother pulling her truck to a stop in front of the kitchen, the shop where she made and sold her different pastries, jams, and jellies, among other things.

Her mother rolled down the window. "Teddie! Come help me!"

Maggie was the heart of the Calloway family. She'd grown up in Montana and had been the daughter of a rancher herself, so she understood the struggles her daughters dealt with, especially from a man like the Colonel. She was calm, warm, and intelligent, with an eye for what worked and what didn't work for her small business. Her mother kept her grounded.

Teddie met Maggie at the back of the Ford pickup, and together they unloaded the supplies and took them into the shed.

"Are you going to bake a lot?" Teddie asked. "This is more than you usually order."

"Yes, it is." Maggie grinned. "I thought I'd use some of those frozen cherries to make room in my freezers. Cherry season will be here before we know it, and I need all the space I can get. I've got a list of new recipes I want to make: scones, muffins, even some cookies."

Cherry Ridge was a cattle ranch and a fruit farm—cherries, apples, and pears, though they had more cherry trees than anything. Nothing was better than a Flathead Cherry, and nobody in a hundred-mile radius turned a cherry into something that tasted like heaven the way Maggie Calloway did. Pies, jams, compote, dried cherries, muffins, scones, and a million other things. So many things that Teddie couldn't keep track of it all. Her mother was always in the kitchen, and a weekend didn't go by that she didn't sell out of whatever she made with her cherries.

"You know what? Will you make a pie for the ranch hands?" Teddie suggested. "They'll love it."

A smile spread across Maggie's face. "That is a wonderful idea." She patted Teddie's cheek. "You're good to those boys. I'm sure they appreciate it."

"I hope so." Teddie cleared her throat and glanced at the stable. "Do you need help with anything else?"

Maggie shook her head, already off in thought, planning her baking for the next few days. Teddie kissed her mother's cheek and resumed her walk to the barn. She didn't see Wyatt right away, so she headed for the opposite end of the barn to see her horse. By the time she slipped inside, Wyatt had emerged from his office and was talking to some of the ranch hands with his back to her.

She couldn't help but stare at him. Wyatt was cowboy through and through—broad shoulders wrapped in a navy blue button-down that clung to every muscle, including his powerful arms and a lean, muscular body formed from years of hard ranch work. She saw his dark brown hair curling under the weight of the Stetson on his head, one he wore more than he didn't. He was perpetually tan, thanks to working outside, and he wore the usual uniform of jeans and work boots. Wyatt had an easy, pleasant smile and a wickedly evil smirk that made her knees go weak. He moved with grace and purpose, like a wolf on the prowl, and when he looked at her, her knees trembled, her heart pounded, and she forgot how to breathe. The man had a body built for sin.

Wyatt had been her weakness since high school. He'd worked at Cherry Ridge for as long as she could remember, and she'd had a crush on him since she was a freshman and he was a senior. For years, she'd hung around the barn, hoping to get his attention.

Not that Wyatt gave her the time of day; Colonel Calloway had a strict "the staff isn't allowed to mingle with the family" rule, an ironclad law he wrote in their contracts. It kept everyone away from his daughters.

"What are you doing down here?"

Teddie jumped and gave Wyatt a sheepish grin. She'd been so caught up in her thoughts, she hadn't realized he was in front of her.

"I wanted to talk to you about moving the cattle," she replied.

Wyatt rolled his eyes. "Christ, not you, too. Everett just yelled at me about it. It's going to take a few days to get everything together, but I will do my best to bring the cattle down off the mountainside by the end of next week."

She narrowed her eyes. "What are you talking about?"

"Your father said he wants the cattle off the mountain as soon as possible," he explained.

"Did he say why?"

Wyatt shook his head. "You didn't know about this, did you?"

"No," Teddie snapped. "Why the hell does he want to bring them down early? We've never done that before."

"Hey, don't yell at me. It wasn't my idea. I wanted to wait until after Labor Day, when it's a little cooler."

"Which is what we usually do, so why does he suddenly want them brought down early?"

Wyatt sighed. "Do not yell at me for this, but he said something about selling them."

"What? No fucking way. We are *not* selling those cattle. We will lose our ass on them." Teddie clenched her fists and swore under her breath.

"I know. I told him that, but he wouldn't listen to me," Wyatt said. "You need to talk to the Colonel."

"I will." She stalked past Wyatt without another word, too angry to even think straight. She needed to find her father and figure out what the hell he was doing.

Teddie rounded the corner in time to see her father and mother driving down the road toward town. So much for talking to him. Maybe it was for the best; it gave her a chance to calm down first. Either she was a part of the business or she wasn't. He couldn't go behind her back and do something as stupid as selling their cattle. It wasn't right, and she intended to talk to him about it. Apparently, she'd have to wait until morning.

With a sigh, she went in the house. She needed a drink.

———

"Where are you going?" her younger sister, Tessa, demanded, standing in front of Teddie's Jeep so she couldn't go anywhere.

"I'm going to town," she replied, leaning out the window. "Do you want to go?"

A smile spread across Tessa's face. "Yes." She danced around the side of the Jeep, yanked open the door, threw her purse on the floor, and got in.

Tessa was twenty-two, a surprise baby who came along when Teddie was eleven. While Teddie carried herself with poise and responsibility—exactly the kind of obedience her father admired—Tessa spoke her mind, embraced her fierce independence, and let her fiery temper and wild streak shine through. She constantly clashed with their father because she refused to conform to his expectations. It wouldn't be long before her sister left Montana behind.

"So, why was Dad pissed off earlier?" Tessa asked.

"Language," Teddie mumbled.

Tessa scowled and tossed her phone on the cupholder between the seats. "I'm twenty-two, Teddie," she groused. "I don't have to watch my language."

"You won't say that if Daddy hears you," she said.

"Colonel Everett Calloway can kiss my ass," Tessa muttered.

Teddie smiled. "Uh oh, what did he do now?"

"Oh, not much, just told me I can't see Noah anymore." Tessa's expression changed, her eyes narrowing and her lips pursing. "He's not good stock, Tessa Jean." Her impersonation of their father was spot-on. "I wish he'd remember we're his daughters, not soldiers for him to command. He's been out of the military for what, almost thirty years?"

Teddie nodded. "Since Grandpa died and left him Cherry Ridge. His attitude won't change, though. Once a military man, always a military man. Now, he's a *rich* military man. Daddy has certain ... ideas about how things work. And he's stubborn. You know that."

Tessa rolled her eyes. "What am I supposed to do about him?"

"What makes you think I know how to deal with him?" Teddie laughed and shook her head.

Tessa sighed. "Oh, I don't know, maybe because you've been around him longer."

"That doesn't mean squat," Teddie muttered. "If it did, you'd be talking to Mom. She's the one who has been married to the man for thirty-five years. I don't know why you think I have it any easier than you do. Daddy controls me as much as he controls you. I don't fight him like you do."

"You should. It'll take some of the heat off me." She crossed her arms and stared out the window. "You know, it would be nice if you rebelled once in a while. I'm sick of carrying the load."

Teddie laughed and shook her head. For a brief second, she considered telling her sister everything, but then she came to her senses. She didn't need the added worry that Tessa would accidentally spill her secret to their father. This secret was one her father would never forgive.

Chapter 2
Wyatt

Wyatt watched Teddie stalk out of the barn, hellbent on finding her father. He felt like a snitch telling her about the cattle, but she was an integral part of the ranch, and he would not lie to her. It was the Colonel's fault for not informing her that he planned to sell the herd.

He wasn't sure why anything the Colonel did surprised him; he'd known the man since he was sixteen, and he hadn't changed one bit. Everett Calloway was demanding, pompous, and difficult to work with. Mostly, he let Teddie and Wyatt take care of the ranch, but now and then, he demanded something ridiculous of them. If he'd let his daughter run the ranch, the place would make money hand over fist.

Despite knowing how difficult the Colonel was to deal with, he'd applied for the head foreman position when it became available three years ago. The pay was good—phenomenal, really—way better than what any other ranch foreman in the Lakeside area received. With good reason. Working for the Colonel was a nightmare.

There were other perks as well, but Wyatt pushed that thought away and set to work feeding the horses, moving from stall to stall, letting himself get lost in his work. It eased his mind and calmed him. He was coming out of the second-to-last stall when he heard his name. He turned to see Luke Moreno walking toward him. Luke was young, in his mid-20s, cocky, but a solid worker.

"Sorry I missed the meeting. Mrs. Calloway asked me to help her get cherries out of the freezer," he said. "What was all that about with the Colonel?"

Wyatt sighed as he walked the length of the barn back to where Luke stood. "He wants us to bring the herd on the mountain down to the bottom pasture."

Luke shrugged. "Yeah, so. We always do that."

"He wants us to do it next week," Wyatt explained.

Luke laughed. "You're joking, right?"

"Unfortunately, no, I'm not joking."

"But that's like three weeks early," Luke muttered. "And this heat wave isn't supposed to break for another couple of weeks."

"I know," Wyatt said. "But he's the boss."

Luke shook his head. "Great. Well, shit. I guess I better enjoy my weekend. Look, I'm gonna head into town. Are you going to the Time Out tonight?"

Wyatt shrugged. "Maybe. I don't know yet. If I do, I plan on beating your ass at pool."

"I'll save you a seat." Luke smiled, tipped his hat, and disappeared through the barn door. Wyatt finished feeding the horses, then he closed up the barn for the night.

He walked outside and leaned on the fence overlooking the pasture. A run-in with both Teddie and her father made for an interesting day. They were so much alike it was scary, not that Teddie or the Colonel would ever admit it.

While he'd known Teddie since high school, he hadn't noticed her until a few years ago. She was a different woman when she returned from college and took over the ranch. She was tall, almost six feet, athletic, and strong from years of working on the ranch. Her honey blonde hair fell to her waist, though she usually kept it in a braid or ponytail. Her green eyes were sharp and observant, filled with quiet determination. She was practical, almost to a fault, but there was a softness to her that few people saw, and those who did thought it meant they could take advantage of her. Definitely not the case. He'd learned that the hard way.

Shortly after Wyatt took over as foreman, he and Teddie had a run-in, of sorts. It was the first time he noticed her as someone more than the Colonel's daughter.

The sun was barely up, the grass still wet with morning dew, when Wyatt spotted Teddie marching across the pasture with a fire in her step and her face etched in anger. She stopped in front of him with her arms crossed.

"You moved the boundary markers," she said.

He didn't bother to look up, just kept hammering, like he hadn't heard the accusatory tone in her voice.

"Good morning, Teddie," he said around a mouthful of nails.

"You shifted the line ten yards to the north."

"Yes, I did," Wyatt replied calmly. "The post was rotting, and the creek is shifting west. You know as well as I do that part of the field floods every spring."

Teddie huffed. "What I know is you didn't ask to move the line."

He took the nails out of his mouth and turned to face her. "I didn't realize I needed to run every fence post movement by the Colonel's daughter."

"Well, maybe you should."

They stared at each other for a long moment, the air between them buzzing with something more electric than the normal indifference they had for each other.

"Do you always get this worked up before breakfast?" Wyatt asked.

"Only when someone redraws the property lines—"

"That is not what I did," he snapped. "I moved the fence line ten yards to the north so I could dig a culvert to keep the pasture from flooding. It is right on the edge of the property line, not past it. Now, if you're done yelling at me, I have work to do."

"Why does everything have to be a fight with you?" she asked.

"I don't want to fight with you, Teddie. I'm trying to keep this place running, like you."

She rolled her eyes. "Fine, next time talk to me first."

"Next time, I will," he said.

Teddie stared at him a beat longer than necessary; then she turned, flipping her blonde hair over her shoulder as she walked away.

Wyatt pinched the bridge of his nose, shaking himself free of the memory. He was tired and ready to go home to his modest cabin at the north end of the ranch. He was halfway to his truck when he turned around, returned to the barn, and went into his office, where he had a fully stocked bathroom and a change of clothes in his bottom drawer. Wyatt cleaned up and changed, then he got in his truck and drove to town. He needed a drink more than he needed sleep.

The Time Out Bar & Grill buzzed with people, like it did most Friday nights. Lakeside College was back in session in less than two weeks, so the college students were coming back to town. Inevitably, their first stop was the hottest hangout in town, the Time Out. It was so busy that Wyatt had to park at Volunteer Park and walk to the bar.

The music hit him as soon as he came through the door. Last spring, the bar's owner, Nate, hired a former rock star to play at the bar—Max Caldwell. Max fell in love with Lakeside—along with Donna, the town sheriff—and ended up staying.

It took Wyatt a few minutes to find the Cherry Ridge crew. They'd commandeered a bunch of seats near the pool tables and were raising hell. It looked like everybody was there—Luke, Hank, Jed, Ty, and Nash, as well as both of the Calloway girls. That wouldn't go over well with Colonel Calloway. He had strict rules about his daughters fraternizing with the hired help.

Wyatt stopped at the bar and got a whiskey before he sauntered over to the group at the pool tables. Luke clapped him on the back before he went back to flirting with Tessa.

Teddie smiled at Wyatt and patted the stool next to her. He sat down and sipped his whiskey.

"Did you talk to your father?" he asked.

She shook her head. "No, my parents left before I had time to ask Daddy about the cattle. I'll talk to him tomorrow."

"Do you think he'll listen to you?"

Teddie snorted. "Does he ever listen to me?"

"Good point," Wyatt muttered. "He doesn't listen to me either."

She bumped her shoulder into his. "Guess we have something in common."

"Wyatt! You're up!"

He got off the stool, tipped his hat, and joined Nash at the pool table. He took the cue, noticing as he bent over that Teddie was watching him. Wyatt winked at her and hit the ball.

Chapter 3
Teddie

He tasted like whiskey, the cheap, good kind that you could only get at the bar, the kind her father would never, ever have in his home. His kisses were wet, sloppy, and damn near perfect. The touch of his rough, calloused hands as they slowly drifted up her sides ignited a fire under her skin. Every inch of her burned with need for him, want and desire woven into every fiber of her being.

Teddie pulled away. "Let's take this somewhere else before someone sees us." She chanced a look around the bar, but she didn't see anybody she knew, at least not in the general vicinity. That didn't mean somebody wouldn't stumble on them in the back corner of the bar where they'd been hiding for the last half an hour, making out like a couple of horny teenagers.

This corner of the Time Out Bar & Grill was dark, buried in the shadows. The jukebox was only a few feet away; the beat of the song thumping in her head and pounding through her blood, filling her brain with all kinds of not-safe-for-work ideas. She'd been thinking about this—about him—all night, ever since he'd walked through the door. Teddie wanted to be alone with him, behind closed doors, in bed.

Wyatt nuzzled her ear with his nose. "Where exactly do you want to go?"

"My place?"

He snorted. "What about your father?"

She laughed. "That didn't seem to bother you two weeks ago when you snuck into my room."

"Yeah, well, I was a nervous wreck the entire time."

Teddie kissed the corner of his mouth and ran her hand up his thigh. "You sure didn't act nervous."

Wyatt closed his eyes and sighed. She bit her lip so she wouldn't laugh again. He couldn't resist her, and she knew it. He'd cave and go back to the ranch with her if she was persuasive enough.

"My father won't even know. Sneak in the back like last time." She pressed her mouth to his ear. "Come home with me. I want you in my bed."

He groaned, then his lips were on her neck, sucking and biting, marking her as he slipped his hand back under her shirt and cupped her breast, his thumb drifting over the nipple.

Teddie's back arched, pushing against his hand, her fingers gripping the waistband of his jeans in a vain attempt to pull him closer.

"I'm not leaving here alone," she whispered. She released his waistband and ran her hand over the front of his jeans, his arousal jumping under her touch, making him groan again.

Wyatt released her, pushing himself into the corner of the booth. "We can't leave at the same time."

Teddie grinned. She had him. "No, of course not. Besides, my sister came with me. I'll get her and we'll leave. I'll leave my French doors unlocked for you."

He smirked, the look making her want to fall to her knees. "Why can't I resist you?" he murmured.

She giggled, kissed him one last time, then she pushed herself out of the booth. "I'll see you in a while."

Teddie went in search of her sister, finding her on the dance floor with Luke, of all people. Great, another Calloway daughter socializing with one of the ranch hands. They were going to give their father a heart attack. She poked her sister in the side and gestured at the door. Tessa rolled her eyes, but she followed Teddie outside.

"We're leaving?" Tessa asked.

"Um, yeah, I have to get up early tomorrow."

To her surprise, Tessa didn't argue. She climbed in the Jeep, shut the door, and made herself comfortable.

Teddie saw it as soon as she rounded the corner and pulled into the driveway. At first, it was a giant, hulking shape in the distance. As they got closer, it took shape—an RV the size of a tour bus parked next to the barn.

Tessa sat forward in her seat and stared at it. "What the hell is that?"

"I do not know," Tessa replied.

"You don't... you don't think that monstrosity belongs to Mom and Dad, do you? Is that what they went to town to pick up earlier?"

"It couldn't be anybody else's," Teddie said. "Not unless a rock star moved into the barn."

"Oh my God, it's hideous. What were they thinking?"

Teddie parked at the head of the driveway. "Trust me, I'm going to find out."

The house was dark when they went inside, so they were careful not to make too much noise, going through the side entrance directly into the kitchen.

"Thanks for letting me go with you," Tessa whispered. "I needed a night out."

Teddie smiled and giggled. Tessa always needed a night out. She squeezed Tessa's arm. "You're welcome."

They separated in the kitchen, each going to their rooms in different parts of the house. When Teddie was in high school, her parents allowed her to move to the "other side of the house," as they called it. Instead of her room being upstairs and down the hall from her parents' room, she was downstairs on the opposite side of the house in what had once been a guest suite. It was a large bedroom with an en suite bathroom and a small sitting area. Teddie tried to lie to herself and say it was almost like having her own place.

When Tessa was home from school, Teddie spent a lot of time in her room. Listening to her father and sister argue about everything drove her insane. Inevitably, Tessa dragged Teddie into every conversation, using her as an example of everything Tessa didn't want to be: the daughter who came home from college to help run the multi-million dollar a year ranch, slept in her teenage bedroom, and followed Daddy's rules.

I don't follow all of Daddy's rules.

Teddie pushed the stupid RV parked outside out of her mind, grabbed a clean set of sheets from her closet, quickly stripped the bed, and remade it. Then she unlocked her French doors, peeled off her clothes, went to the bathroom, and took a shower to wash off the bar smell. When she was done, she went to the bed, sighing as she sank into its inviting softness.

On the other side of the room, one of the double doors opened, and Wyatt slipped inside. A smile spread across his face as he crossed the room, his nimble fingers swiftly unbuttoning his long-sleeved button-down, leaving him in a plain white T-shirt and his low-slung jeans. He kicked off his boots, and then he was on her, pinning her beneath him on the bed.

Yeah, I definitely don't follow all of Daddy's rules.

—

Teddie straddled the man sleeping in her bed, tugged the oversized shirt she wore—his, of course—up around her waist, and pressed a kiss to the center of his back, right between his shoulder blades.

Wyatt stirred, groaning as he glanced back at her. "Hey. What time is it?"

"Five," she murmured.

"Shit." He moaned and buried his face in the pillow.

Teddie laughed and ducked under his arm, forcing him to roll to his side so she could snuggle up to him. His heavy hand fell on her waist, and his knee pushed between her legs as he pulled her close, tucking her beneath his chin.

She sighed and rested her head on his chest, his heart thumping in her ear. She wanted to stay there forever.

"I should go," Wyatt whispered.

Before she could protest, he slid out from under her and picked up his boots and jeans. He quickly put them on, then he turned to her with a smirk on his face.

"I need my shirt."

Teddie laughed as she got up and kneeled in front of him. She grabbed the hem of the shirt and pulled it over her head, holding it out to him with what she hoped was an innocent smile on her face, even though she felt anything but innocent.

Wyatt shook his head, his blue eyes flashing, and snatched the shirt from her hands. He put it on, then he grabbed Teddie, lifting her off the bed. His hands were hot against her naked skin as he pulled her legs around his waist. His mouth covered hers, and he kissed her as if he had no intention of leaving.

"Don't go," she said, running her fingers through his hair, her lips drifting along his jaw.

Wyatt sighed. "I have to. If your father finds me in here, he'll kill me." He set her on the bed, kissed her once more, and then he was gone.

Teddie crawled back under the covers and stared at the door. Unfortunately, he was correct; her father would kill Wyatt if he found him in Teddie's room.

Teddie put her hands over her face and groaned. What the hell was she doing? Of all the rules she and Wyatt decided to break, it had to be the one Everett Calloway was most adamant about.

———

Teddie poured herself another cup of coffee and went in search of her father. While she was still angry about the sale of the cattle, she'd calmed down enough to discuss it with him rationally. There was also the question of the RV. Everett was on the porch with Maggie, having breakfast.

She slipped into the chair beside her mother and set her cup on the table.

"Good morning," Maggie said, reaching over to squeeze Teddie's hand. "You and Tessa were out late. Did you go into town?"

Teddie nodded. "To the Time Out."

Out of the corner of her eye, she saw her father roll his eyes. She ignored it.

"So, what's with the giant bus by the barn?" Teddie asked. "Did we adopt a rock star?"

Maggie glanced at her husband, then back at Teddie. "Your father purchased an RV. We… we're going to travel."

"Travel? In that?"

"Yes." Maggie looked at Everett and her daughter. "I'm going down to the shop. You two play nice." She patted Teddie's hand, kissed Everett's cheek, and left them to talk.

"Did you have something to say, young lady?" Everett asked.

"Yes." Teddie cleared her throat. "Why are you selling the cattle?"

"Who told you?"

"So, you're not denying it?" Teddie sighed.

"Yes, I'm selling the cattle. Now, who told you?"

"Wyatt. He told me yesterday."

Everett chuckled. "And you waited until today to ask? That's not like you."

"I needed time to calm down," she snapped. She closed her eyes and took a deep breath. "This will seriously hurt Cherry Ridge. I'm guessing you're selling them below market price, is that right?"

"Correct."

"Daddy, you understand that selling those cattle will cost us up to $500,000. Right?"

"I am aware."

Teddie jumped up, the chair wobbling slightly before righting itself. "Then why are you doing it? And why didn't you tell me?"

"I don't have to tell you everything," Everett muttered.

"I think you do. Because this ranch is my life. I gave up everything to come back here and help you run it. I need to be included in a major decision like this."

Everett pinched the bridge of his nose and sighed. "I hoped to put this conversation off for a while."

Teddie narrowed her eyes. "What conversation?"

Her father shifted uncomfortably and stared at a spot above her head for almost thirty seconds before he answered.

"I'm selling the ranch."

Her world tilted on its axis, the words "selling the ranch" ringing in her ears like the echo of a gunshot. She gripped the table to keep herself upright as her stomach twisted and vomit rose in the back of her throat. A sudden aching pressure exploded in her chest. She swallowed, but her throat was tight and raw.

"You're... you're selling Cherry Ridge?"

Everett nodded. "Yes. Your mother and I aren't getting any younger. We'd like to enjoy our remaining years without the burden of running the ranch. That's why I bought the RV, so we can travel and see the sights. Selling the cattle is the first step toward the end goal. I have a buyer for the cattle, and the same person is interested in purchasing Cherry Ridge."

"But... but this place has been in our family for generations. You *can't* sell it."

"This is for the best, Theodora. You never wanted this life, anyway. I'm giving you a chance at freedom, a chance to live your life like you've always wanted. I won't let you carry the burden of Cherry Ridge."

A dull roar filled her ears as he spoke until all she heard was the blood pounding through her veins. She had worked on the ranch since she was a little girl, learned every inch, bled for it, given up everything for it. Did he really think she could walk away?

"No," she murmured. Teddie cleared her throat. "You can't sell it. Cherry Ridge belongs to our family. It's my legacy. It's not a burden. You can't take it away from me."

"While I appreciate your sentimental ties to the ranch, I've made my decision. We're not discussing it any further." Everett checked his watch. "Now, if you'll excuse me, I have a meeting."

Teddie sank slowly back into her chair as he stalked off, shoulders stiff, fists clenched at his sides. An immense sense of loss fell over her, so deep and gut-wrenching she had to bite her lip to hold back the tears. Her father had destroyed her life and walked away like it was no big deal.

She allowed herself a moment to grieve—no longer— then she squared her shoulders and rose to her feet. It would be a snowy day in hell before she let Cherry Ridge go.

Not without a fight.

Chapter 4
Wyatt

Wyatt hurried down the hill behind the house, cut through the cherry orchard, and headed for the barn. On the way, he grabbed clean clothes from the truck so he could shower and change. It wouldn't be the first time he'd done it since he started seeing Teddie.

If someone had told him a year ago, he would be dating—and seriously in love with—his boss's daughter, he'd have laughed in their face. But, after a drunken one-night stand and the best sex he ever had, fast forward almost a year, and he was in a position he never imagined himself in.

The Calloway women were strictly off-limits; they always had been. He'd known that since he started working at Cherry Ridge when he was sixteen, and he never thought twice about it. That rule had not changed.

A half an hour later, Wyatt had showered and put on clean clothes, and he was at his desk with a cup of coffee in his hand, going over paperwork and worrying about getting the herd of cattle moved down the mountain. It made his head hurt thinking about it.

"I recognize that face," a familiar voice said from the open office door. "You're figuring something out and it's kicking your ass."

"Jesse? What the hell are you doing here?" Wyatt laughed as he pushed himself out of his chair and hurried across the room, hand extended.

They met in the middle of the room, exchanging a handshake and a quick hug. Jesse McBride was one of his oldest and closest friends. The two men had known each other for years, attending both high school and college together before returning to Lakeside. But they had gone to work for rival ranches; Wyatt at Cherry Ridge and Jesse for Remington Cattle.

"I'm here to look at the herd," Jesse replied. "Remington wants to buy them. Preston brought me because that idiot knows absolutely nothing about cattle. Since I was here, I thought I'd stop by and say hello. It's been a while."

They chatted for a few before Jesse shook Wyatt's hand and excused himself. Wyatt leaned against his desk, the headache roaring between his ears. A soft whinny drew his attention, reminding him he still needed to feed the horses. He left his office, grabbed a bucket, and went to work. It took him almost an hour to make his way down the stalls. By the time he got to the last one, he was ready for a cup of coffee.

"Hi," a voice whispered inches away from his ear, making him jump.

"Jesus Christ, Teddie," he huffed. "You scared the shit out of me." He put the bucket of oats in front of the chestnut mare in the stall's corner.

Teddie grinned. "Sorry." She stepped into him, pushed herself up on her toes, put her hands on his waist, and kissed him on the corner of the mouth.

"What are you doing in here?" Wyatt tried to sound stern, but he failed.

"I wanted to see you." She slid her arms around him as she stepped closer, her body flush against his.

"You're lucky your father didn't see you," he said.

"He won't," Teddie shot back. "I've gotten really good at this."

Wyatt chuckled and shook his head. They had both gotten surprisingly good at sneaking around over the last six months. He glanced at the stall door, then he cupped Teddie's chin in his hand, tilted her head back, and kissed her. What he really wanted to do was throw her in the hay and take her, a plan he was sure she would have been one hundred percent on board with, but he held himself in check by sheer force of will.

Teddie drove him crazy and made him throw his inhibitions right out the window, including the one about staying away from the boss's daughter.

"Stop that," she scolded, punching him on the arm.

"Stop what?"

"Stop overthinking this and us." She wrapped a hand around the back of his neck and pulled him back to her lips, her tongue drifting over his and sliding into his mouth. She pushed into the kiss, her breasts pressing against his chest, her body warm, supple, and soft.

Reluctantly, Wyatt pushed her away and took a step back. "Did you talk to your father about the cattle sale yet?"

She nodded. "Yes, and I have a lot to tell you. Why?"

"Because Preston Remington is here with their foreman to look at the herd."

"What? He's here?"

Wyatt nodded. "Yeah, Jesse stopped to say hello and mentioned why they were here."

"Shit. I gotta go." She darted out of the stall and took off at a run for the path that circled the house, leading to the converted guesthouse around the back.

He was glad he didn't have to deal with an angry Teddie. When she got mad, she became a force to be reckoned with. And she was absolutely fuming.

Ten minutes later, Jesse strolled into the barn.

"Well, that was interesting," he said.

"What was interesting?" Wyatt asked, grabbing his coffee off his workbench.

"I don't remember Teddie Calloway being such a take-charge person," Jesse explained. "I remember a quiet, mousy girl who had a massive crush on you in high school."

Wyatt laughed. "That was fifteen years ago. Don't mess with her. She knows her shit. Do you know she got the ranch running in the black for four years straight? I think she can run this ranch better than anyone. Teddie knows this place inside and out; she knows what works and what doesn't. She's smart when it comes to doing what needs to be done."

Jesse raised an eyebrow. "How long have you been sleeping with her?"

Wyatt spat out the coffee he was swallowing. "What are you talking about?"

"I have known you since we were kids, Wyatt. You can't fool me. You've got it bad for that woman."

"Is it that obvious?" Wyatt asked.

"Does she know?"

Wyatt laughed. "Dude, we've been seeing each other for months."

Jesse's eyes widened. "Does the Colonel know?"

"Hell, no! Do not say anything to him. Or to Preston. That asshole will go running to the Colonel and rat us out faster than he sucks down one of his stupid cigarettes."

Jesse held up his hands and chuckled. "Okay, okay. I won't say a word. I swear. But I gotta ask. Is it serious?"

Wyatt shrugged. "We've never talked about it. Do I want it to be serious? Maybe. And I think Teddie does, too."

The sound of voices coming toward them ended that conversation, which didn't bother Wyatt. He hadn't talked to Teddie about their relationship and where they stood, so he wasn't comfortable talking to Jesse about it.

Wyatt leaned against the wall and crossed his arms. "I don't suppose you have a few men to spare next week?"

"Why? What's up?"

"I'm bringing the herd down off the mountain, and I need a few extra hands," Wyatt explained. "If I have some extra men, I might keep people from getting overheated."

"Why don't you wait until it cools down?"

Wyatt rolled his eyes. "The Colonel wants them off the mountain ASAP."

Jesse chuckled. "Of course he does." He tapped his chin. "I can spare at least two ranch hands. Plus, me."

"You don't have to do that," Wyatt said.

"I want to," Jesse said. "Besides, we don't currently have any cattle, the hay is cut and stored, and my list of chores is short. I've got time."

Teddie marched toward him, Preston right behind her. Her tight lips and angry stance told him everything he needed to know. This was going to be interesting.

Chapter 5

Teddie

"Daddy?" Teddie called.

She slammed the door shut behind herself and propped her sunglasses on top of her head.

"Daddy?" she shouted again.

"In my office," he bellowed.

The Colonel's office was at the back of the guest house, in what had once been the master bedroom. As Teddie rounded the corner, she ran directly into Preston Remington. He caught her as she stumbled, one hand on her waist, the other gripping her upper arm. He smiled, his face inches from hers.

"Teddie. How are you?"

She sighed and disentangled herself from Preston's grip. "Hello, Preston. What are you doing here?"

"Discussing business with your father," he replied. "Nothing you need to worry about."

Teddie rolled her eyes. It didn't surprise her he hadn't told the truth. The man was allergic to it. Besides, he knew as well as she did that she understood the business better than her father, who was nothing more than a figurehead. Wyatt ran the day-to-day operations of the ranch, and she dealt with everything else. Everett discussing anything with Preston was laughable. She definitely knew more than a snotty trust fund baby did about running a ranch.

"What kind of business?" she asked, wondering if he would be honest with her.

Her father stepped out of his office. "I told you. Preston is interested in buying the cattle along with the ranch. But he wants to look at them first."

"They're still on the mountain," Teddie said.

"Not the ones in the south pasture," Everett replied calmly. "Why don't you grab the Jeep and take Preston out there?"

Her father had a glint in his eye, the one she knew meant he had been scheming and plotting. He'd had the same look when he encouraged her to move back home and work at the ranch. There was something he wasn't telling her.

"I have work to do," Teddie argued.

"It can wait," the Colonel said. "Go with Preston and check out the cattle. Maybe run it by Wyatt, because he knows the herd better than any of us.

She bit back the "No shit," on her lips and gave her father a dirty look before she followed Preston out of the office. She put her sunglasses on, pushed past Preston, and stalked toward the barn with Preston hot on her heels, chattering in her ear, the scent of tobacco floating from the cigarette he'd lit as soon as they'd left the guest house.

Fuming over her father's interference in what she felt was *her* ranch, she heard nothing Preston said. They were almost at the barn when he grabbed her arm and stopped her.

"What?" she snapped.

"I asked if you wanted to get lunch later," he said.

Teddie shook off the hand on her arm and stepped away from him. God, she hated this. Preston had always had a crush on her, ever since high school. While he was nice enough—for a spoiled rich kid who wanted for nothing and whose father doted on him until his death three years ago—he wasn't her type, something he didn't seem to understand. For two years, he'd followed her around like a lost puppy, repeatedly asking her out, refusing to accept that she didn't reciprocate his feelings. After high school, they both went off to different colleges, and Teddie hoped he would move on. But now and then, Preston turned up, asked her out, she turned him down, and life resumed. Hopefully, this would be another one of those times.

"I don't think so."

Preston shook his head, chuckling under his breath. "Are you still playing hard to get?"

"I never played hard to get," Teddie snapped. "I am not interested in dating you."

"Your father said you don't have a boyfriend," he replied.

She rolled her eyes. "He told you that?"

He shrugged. "Maybe he thought you might go out with me."

Teddie pushed a hand through her hair and quelled the urge to yank it out in frustration. "Just because my father said it doesn't mean it's true. He knows nothing about my personal life. Or my love life."

Preston shrugged. "We'll see." He walked past her toward the barn, flicking his still lit cigarette butt on the ground.

She clenched her fists as she snorted, put her heel on Preston's cigarette butt, and ground it into the dirt. Out of the corner of her eye, she saw Wyatt and the foreman from Remington Ranch, Jesse McBride, leaning against the stable wall. Preston called Jesse's name. Teddie picked up the pace, arriving at the barn a few seconds after Preston.

"Thanks, Jesse," Wyatt said, shaking his friend's hand. "I appreciate your help. It will be tight, but I think we'll make it." He tipped his chin in her direction as she approached. "Ms. Calloway, what brings you out this early? Are you looking to ride your favorite stallion?" He winked at her, making her blush.

Teddie took a deep breath and glared at Wyatt. "I need the Jeep. I'm taking Preston and Jesse to look at the cattle in the south pasture."

Preston put his hand in the middle of her back and grinned at Wyatt. "Then we're going to lunch." He slipped his arm around her waist, pulling her tight against his side.

Wyatt nodded, an odd look falling over his face. "The Jeep is behind the barn. If you'll excuse me, I need to get back to work."

Teddie took a step toward him. "Wyatt—"

Wyatt didn't look at her; he just disappeared back into the stables.

———

Teddie, Preston, and Jesse were out on the southernmost part of the property for close to two hours, discussing the cattle and the sale of the ranch. She didn't agree with the terms, and she told Preston as much, a concept he had a difficult time grasping. He argued with her all the way back to the main house, doing his best to convince her it was in the best interest of everyone involved for the Calloways to sell their herd along with the ranch.

"We stand to lose thousands of dollars," Teddie argued. "I do not see how this is a viable option for us. I need to discuss this with my father."

As soon as Jesse parked the Jeep in front of the house, Teddie had the door open and her feet on the pavement. Preston jumped out after her and followed her up the porch steps to the front door, where she stopped.

"What are you doing?" she asked.

"I thought we could talk about it some more over lunch," Preston replied. He took a drag of his cigarette, blowing smoke in her face as he exhaled.

Teddie clenched her fists. His chain-smoking was getting on her nerves. "I don't think so. We've discussed all that needs to be discussed. I'm going to talk to my father and make sense of this nonsense, then I'll be in touch. Have a good day." She opened the door, stepped inside, and slammed the door in Preston's face.

She walked through the house, out the back door, and down the short path to the converted guest house. Her father wasn't inside, and when she called his cell phone, he didn't answer. She dropped into the chair at her desk and put her head in her hands.

Maybe it was a good thing the Colonel wasn't around. Teddie was still furious with him. She turned on her computer and ran the numbers. By the time she finished, she was even more frustrated.

If her calculations were right—and they usually were—they might lose close to $500,000 if the Remingtons stuck to their offer, which was far below the expected market value for both the ranch and the cattle. The ranch was worth millions, and Preston was lowballing them.

"My father has lost his mind," she muttered out loud as she pushed her chair away from the desk. Her head pounded from staring at her computer screen. She needed some air.

Teddie followed the path down to the stables, one of her favorite places on the ranch. She loved how quiet it was, the only sounds the gentle neighing of the horses and the rustling of them moving in their stalls. She stopped outside Wild Blue's stall and waited. It only took a second for the horse to notice her, a soft whinny leaving him as he put his head over the stall door and nudged her hand.

"Hey, Blue," she whispered, scratching his chin. "How are you, buddy?"

"He missed you."

Teddie jumped, her heart hammering in her chest. She rested her forehead against Blue's broad face for a moment before she turned to the man standing beside her.

"I missed him." She wasn't talking about the horse, and she didn't think Wyatt had been either.

"How was lunch?" Wyatt asked.

She heard the jealousy in his voice, though she was pretty sure he tried to hide it. Why couldn't he understand he had nothing to worry about, no need to be jealous, because her heart belonged to one man and one man only? Not that she'd ever said the words. She'd never told him she loved him, thanks to the underlying fear of her father and what he would do to Wyatt if he found out. The fear was always there, creeping around the back of her mind, dictating everything she did.

"I didn't go to lunch." She stepped away from Wild Blue, put her arms around Wyatt, and rested her head on his shoulder. His familiar, warm, and comforting scent washed over her, making her heady with desire.

"You didn't?" he whispered.

"Nope." Teddie smiled at him, plucked the hat from his head, and ran her fingers through his hair, scratching at the short hairs on the back of his neck as she pulled him down to meet her lips.

That simple kiss ignited the spark. Wyatt's arms locked around her waist as he dragged her into his office and slammed the door shut, drawing a few startled neighs from the horses. Teddie didn't know whether to melt with need or giggle at the craziness of what they were doing.

He pushed her against the door, impatient and greedy, his mouth slanted over hers, devouring her like a starving man as he maneuvered his thigh between her legs, pressing it against her warm core.

His name was a curse on her lips as she fumbled to undo his belt and pull open his pants. Wyatt groaned as her fingers brushed his half-hard cock.

He reached around her and flipped the lock on the door, then he picked Teddie up and carried her across the room to his desk, balancing her on the edge. Wyatt tugged her shirt up, his hands sliding beneath it to cup her breasts, his thumbs tracing her nipples through her lace bra.

She moaned, her back arching and her head falling back as his lips drifted along the line of her throat. She shoved her hand into the waistband of his underwear and took hold of his length, stroking him gently. His hips thrust with the movements as he impatiently pulled at her clothes; her shirt and bra effortlessly removed and tossed aside.

Wyatt stepped back, his blue eyes darkening with lust as he watched her take off her boots. He helped her yank her jeans off, both of them panting with lust by the time she was free of the tight denim. He pushed open her thighs and stepped between them, his hand between her legs, his fingers teasing her, opening her for him.

Teddie pushed his jeans and underwear down past his ass, and she guided him into her, hissing as the burn of the stretch balanced her perfectly on the edge between pleasure and pain. She wrapped her arms around him, put her hands on his ass, and urged him to move. It was all hands, lips, her and Wyatt, connected in the most intimate of ways, his body flush against hers, his mouth on hers, kissing her senseless, swallowing her moans as she climaxed, the orgasm exploding out of her, consuming her, a never ending moment in time that she didn't want to end.

Wyatt's orgasm came shortly after hers, his whole body tensing and his blunt fingertips digging into her hips as he came. When it was over, he rested his head on her shoulder, his breath tearing in and out of his throat.

The knock on the door startled both of them. Her hand hit a box of paperclips, knocking them to the floor.

"Dawson? Are you in there?" Another sharp knock.

"Shit," Wyatt swore under his breath, pushed himself away from her, and yanked his jeans up.

Teddie jumped off the desk and scrambled to grab her clothes. Then she ran for the bathroom, shutting the door a few seconds before Wyatt opened his office door.

"Colonel Calloway," Teddie heard Wyatt say. "What can I do for you?"

Chapter 6

Wyatt

Wyatt buckled his belt, glanced over his shoulder at the now-closed bathroom door, then he yanked open his office door.

"Colonel Calloway. What can I do for you?"

Everett pushed past him, marched into the office, and stopped in the middle of the room with his arms crossed. He glanced slowly around, his eyes stopping on Wyatt.

"You need to clean up in here," Everett muttered.

Wyatt sighed. "Yes, sir."

"Where are we with moving the cattle down from the mountain?" Everett asked.

"We're leaving the day after tomorrow," Wyatt explained. "Jesse McBride from Remington Ranch is going to help."

"How long will it take?"

"Two days at least," he replied. "Or three. And no, I can't do it any faster. I don't want to lose any cattle or chance anybody getting heatstroke."

Everett scowled. "Whatever. Get them moved ASAP." He stormed out of the office without another word.

The bathroom door opened, and Teddie peered out. "Is he gone?"

Wyatt nodded and leaned against the edge of his desk as Teddie came out, fully dressed.

"I'm going with you," she said.

"What?" he asked. "Going where with me?"

"To get the cattle," she replied.

"Absolutely not."

Teddie crossed her arms and scowled, the look on her face surprisingly like her father's. "What do you mean, absolutely not? This is my ranch. I go where I please."

Wyatt rubbed his forehead. Everett would lose his shit when he found out Teddie planned to join them when they went to get the cattle. But Wyatt wasn't about to argue with her. He wouldn't win, anyway.

"Alright, we're leaving at six a.m. sharp, day after tomorrow."

"I'll be ready." She went to the door, stopped with her hand on the doorknob, and looked back at him. "I'll tell my father so you don't have to. See you later."

"Bye," he mumbled as the door swung closed behind her.

———

Teddie was already outside the barn with Blue saddled when Wyatt came around the corner. She threw her backpack in the back of the truck with the other supplies, then leaned against it with that look on her face that made him want to rip off her clothes. It wasn't just the Colonel who wouldn't like Teddie going with them to round up the cattle. That woman was temptation wrapped up in tight jeans and a pair of cowboy boots.

Wyatt gave her a tight smile, tossed his duffle in the truck's bed, and hurried inside to get his horse out of her stall. He was going to stay as far away from Teddie as possible, otherwise, God only knew what he might do.

"You ready for this?"

He jumped, swung around, and glared at Teddie. She wasn't going to make it easy on him, that was for sure.

"What is wrong with you?"

"Nothing," he muttered.

"Something must be bothering you," she replied.

"I said nothing," Wyatt reiterated. "Are you set to go?"

She nodded. "I brought my tent, too, like you said."

"Good," he said. He took a deep breath and exhaled. "Thanks."

Teddie nodded and followed him out of the barn. Wyatt finished saddling his horse, then he asked everyone to gather around.

"Good morning, everybody," Wyatt said. "Thanks for being here. I know we usually do this after Labor Day when it's cooler, but the Colonel asked us to bring the cattle down early, so that's what we're going to do. I'd also like to thank Jesse and the crew from Remington Ranch for offering to help. You guys know the drill. Hank will take the road up the side of the mountain, and the rest of us are heading up on the horses. We'll camp at our usual spot tonight and start bringing the cattle down tomorrow. Questions?"

Wyatt wasn't surprised there weren't questions. He'd worked with this crew for several years, and they could do this with their eyes closed. The only newbie, so to speak, was Teddie. Not that anyone would dare say anything to her about it.

It took most of the day to get up the side of the mountain to their camping spot, less than half a mile from the cattle. Hank was there with the truck and the dogs, the tents set up, and two fires roaring. He'd driven the uneven, bumpy trail up to the campsite, a trail that wound around the mountain and couldn't be used to bring the cattle down. After they fed, watered, and tethered the horses for the night, everyone pitched in to help cook dinner. By the time they ate and cleaned up, the sun was setting.

Wyatt noticed Teddie walk off through the trees after everyone grabbed beers and took a seat. He excused himself, snatched two beers from the cooler as he walked by it, and followed her. He found her sitting on a rock, looking out over a valley that stretched to Flathead Lake, so he sat down beside her and held out the beer. She took it with a smile.

"Thanks," she murmured. She took a long swallow, then wiped her mouth with the back of her hand. "It's beautiful, isn't it?"

The valley unfolded below them like a painting, rolling fields and dense clusters of trees woven together like a tapestry of green and gold. Flathead Lake shimmered in the distance, reflecting the reds and oranges of the setting sun. Wyatt dragged in a deep breath, the crisp air clearing his lungs. Sometimes, he forgot to stop and take a breath. Fortunately, Teddie reminded him daily that there was beauty in the world and he needed to take time to admire it.

"It is," he said.

"Cherry Ridge is my favorite place in the entire world. I've loved it since I was a little girl. I know every inch of this place like the back of my own hands. I know I grumble and complain and say that I came back here after college because of my father, but I did it because I love this place. I can't imagine anybody taking care of it like I do." She glanced at Wyatt. "Like you do."

"Was that a compliment, Theodora?" he joked.

After a moment he said, "I love this place, too. I've worked on this ranch since I was sixteen, and I never want to work anyplace else. You know, when I was younger, I used to dream about owning Cherry Ridge."

Teddie sighed and glanced at him out of the corner of her eye. "My father is selling it."

Wyatt wasn't sure he heard right. "What?"

"You heard me," she mumbled. "My father is going to sell Cherry Ridge. He said he doesn't want to burden me with it, and he is ready to move on and live his life. Or something like that. That stuff with Preston wasn't just about the cattle. It's about the whole damn ranch."

"Are you fucking kidding me?" Wyatt shook his head. "Jesus, maybe I'll buy it."

Teddie bumped her shoulder against his. "You'd have to fight me for it."

He chuckled. "I know. I know you love this place as much as I do."

"Almost as much as I love you."

"Wh-what did you say?"

"I said I love you." She laughed and put her hands over her face. "I cannot believe I said that to you out here in the middle of nowhere with eight ranch hands back there waiting for us around the fire. That was not how I wanted to tell you I love you for the first time."

Wyatt took her hand and pressed a quick kiss to her cheek. "I love you, too." He glanced over his shoulder. "And I can't believe I'm saying this, but I should probably get back there around the fire."

"Yeah, you should," she agreed. "I may be in love with you, but I'm not ready for my father to find out. Not yet."

He sighed. "I know. Someday, we'll figure out how I can be good enough for the great Colonel Everett Calloway." He turned to go, but Teddie grabbed his hand.

"Hey. You're good enough for me, Wyatt, and that is what matters."

Wyatt squeezed her hand, then he got up and hurried back to the fire with the others. He had to work to keep the grin off his face.

She loves me.

Chapter 7
Teddie

Teddie stared at the top of her tent and the faint sliver of moonlight making shadows on the tent's walls. She still couldn't believe she'd told Wyatt she loved him. She'd been holding onto that information for weeks, scared to say it out loud because she didn't want to freak him out. When she imagined expressing her feelings to him, it was during some beautiful, candlelit moment. She certainly hadn't intended to tell him out in the middle of a cattle drive with more than half a dozen ranch hands lurking in the dark.

"So much for that idea," she mumbled to herself.

Teddie sat up, unzipped her tent, and peered out. The stars, undisturbed by city lights, shone almost as bright as the moon. Crickets hummed in the tall grass and the embers in the fire crackled on the other side of the camp-site. A cool breeze rolled down the mountain, so she grabbed a blanket, wrapped it around her shoulders, and slipped out of the tent. There were four other tents besides hers; she was the only one who wasn't sharing.

One of the ranch dogs, Echo, looked up when she opened her tent. He padded across the clearing and sat in front of her, his head tipped to one side.

She climbed out, patted Echo on the head, wandered across the campsite, and sat by the fire. Echo lay down beside her, while the other dogs—Kris and Scout—scooted closer to the fire. Teddie absentmindedly rubbed Echo's ears while she stared at the stars overhead.

Even though she hadn't told Wyatt she loved him in exactly the way she'd planned, she was glad she'd done it. Having him say it back to her was an unexpected, head-spinning development. A smile played at the corner of her lips.

Wyatt loves me.

Teddie closed her eyes and breathed deep, the familiar smell of the ranch, of outdoors, of *Montana*, filling her nostrils. God, she loved it out here; there was no better place on earth. How could her father think about selling the ranch?

"There has to be something I can do," she muttered out loud.

"Talking to yourself, sweetheart?" Wyatt said from behind her.

Teddie squeaked, slapping her hand over her mouth to keep it from turning into a full-blown scream, while the dogs growled in unison. She clutched the blanket around her shoulders tighter and swung around. He stood a few feet away in a pair of sweatpants, a thin white T-shirt, and cowboy boots. As soon as the dogs realized it was Wyatt, they wagged their tails.

She looked him up and down, suppressing a giggle. "What are you wearing? Sweatpants and cowboy boots? And what are you doing sneaking around?" she whispered. "I thought you were asleep."

"I couldn't sleep, so I checked on the horses," he replied. "I didn't bring my slippers, and I'm sure the hell not going to walk around barefoot. What are you doing up?"

She shrugged. "I can't sleep. Too much on my mind."

"You worried about tomorrow?" he asked.

Teddie shook her head and scoffed. "No. I can wrangle cattle in my sleep. I've been doing it for years. I have *other* things on my mind."

Wyatt crossed his arms and smirked. "Oh, yeah?"

She was on her feet in an instant and in front of him. "Yes. For instance, I just found out the man I love also loves me. I'm reeling."

He chuckled. "Reeling, huh? What does that look like?"

Teddie glanced at the tents behind Wyatt, stepped into him, and put her arms around his neck. "Like this." She caught his lips in hers and kissed him.

When they broke apart and she stepped back, he grabbed her hand and dragged her across the campsite to her tent. When the dogs tried to follow, he ordered them to stay, which they did.

Teddie crawled inside the tent with Wyatt right behind her. He dropped to his knees, zipped the tent shut, and grabbed Teddie's ankles, pulling her toward him until she was lying flat on her sleeping bag.

"What are you doing?" she whispered, kicking her feet.

"Shh," Wyatt hissed as he ran his hands up her legs, slowly caressing the inside of her thighs.

Teddie sighed and relaxed under his touch as his fingers drifted under the edge of the tight boy shorts she wore, his rough, calloused fingers sending shots of electricity through every inch of her body. A low moan slipped out of her as he brushed her rapidly heating center.

Wyatt stopped and leaned over her, one hand on either side of her head. "If you're not quiet, I'll stop," he whispered. "And believe me, you don't want me to stop."

Teddie nodded as he eased his fingers down the front of her underwear and gently caressed her.

"Okay?" he asked.

She nodded, afraid to speak, because she definitely didn't want him to stop.

Wyatt pushed her T-shirt up past her breasts and captured her nipple in his mouth. His tongue circled the now erect nipple as he continued his exploration of her warm center. When his finger slid into her while his teeth tugged at her nipple, she nearly lost it. He grinned against her skin.

He kissed his way down her stomach until he hovered over her. Teddie grabbed his head with both hands and forced him to look at her.

"Wyatt, no," she whispered, shaking her head. She knew if he did what she knew he was about to do, she wouldn't be able to keep quiet.

"Oh, yes, sweetheart." That gorgeous smirk was back. "Remember, be quiet." He winked, his eyes on her as he pulled off her underwear and tossed them aside. Then, he slowly licked her.

Another moan rose in her chest, so she slapped her hand over her mouth, barely able to contain it. Her head fell back, waves of pleasure washing over her as Wyatt went to work. His tongue slid into her, along with his finger. He moved them together, his finger crooking just right to hit that perfect, sweet spot. The orgasm built in the pit of her stomach, and then she exploded, heat rushing through her as she rode out the insanity of the climax. A quiet whimper escaped her.

Wyatt pulled away and once again hovered over her. "I told you to be quiet." He kissed her, the taste of her on his tongue making her dizzy with desire.

Teddie pushed at his sweatpants, desperate to touch him. He sat up and shoved them off, along with his boxers and T-shirt. She took him in her hand and caressed his hard length, causing his breath to catch in his throat. He closed his eyes, bit his lip, and groaned.

"Shh," Teddie murmured.

He grinned at her, then he kissed her, sucking her lower lip as he pushed her legs apart and settled between them, his cock nestled at her entrance. The kiss continued as he slowly entered her, inch by glorious inch.

Unable to control herself, she moaned Wyatt's name. He thrust deep into her, hard, deliberately. She almost lost her mind as she kept pace with him, thrust for thrust, her hips snapping up to meet his, her nails scratching at his back.

It didn't take long for the familiar tension to rise in her again, her climax building and building as she desperately choked back the scream of pleasure attempting to burst free.

Wyatt knew how close she was, because he put his hand over her mouth, and God dammit, he stopped the delicious movement of his hips. He wrapped his other arm around her back and held her close as he looked into her eyes.

"I want you to cum for me, baby. I want you to cum all over my cock."

His hips twitched, and Teddie thought she might faint from the overwhelming sensations coursing through her. Her eyes rolled back in her head, and she sighed against his hand. Wyatt pulled his hand away, put his finger to his lips, then he sat up on his knees, moving her so her hips rose off the ground to meet his. He pulled her toward him at the same time that he furiously pounded into her.

It only took several perfectly placed thrusts before she came undone, the tension uncoiling inside her and the undeniable bliss exploding through her entire body as she rode out her orgasm.

Wyatt stiffened, and then his own climax took him, eliciting a satisfied grunt from him. He fell forward, catching himself with his hands next to her head. He kissed her before he collapsed next to her.

"Fuck, Teddie, that was amazing," he whispered.

A shiver rushed through her, though she wasn't sure if it was because of Wyatt or the chill night air. He must have noticed, because he got up, maneuvered her into the sleeping bag, and zipped her up before putting his clothes back on. He kissed her forehead, whispered, "I love you," and then he was gone.

"I love you, too," she said after him.

Chapter 8

Wyatt

Wyatt was up first, before the sun, stoking the flames of the fire to start breakfast and make coffee. He couldn't help but glance at Teddie's tent now and then, wondering how she slept after he left her.

"Mornin' Wyatt," Jesse called.

He raised a hand and waved at his friend, then went back to making coffee. It was going to be a long day, and he wanted to get moving before the heat overtook them.

The tents slowly emptied as everyone got up, ready to start the day. Wyatt left Hank to deal with the coffee and breakfast to look for Luke and Ty. He found them saddling their horses under the trees.

"Good morning," he said. "Did you boys eat breakfast?"

"Yes, sir," Ty replied with a grin.

Wyatt liked Ty; he was young, barely twenty, eager to please, and smart enough to make a split-second decision if necessary. He knew he wouldn't have Ty around long because someone was bound to snatch him up for a foreman job.

"I want you two to take the dogs and go up the mountain. You need to make sure we've got a clear path to the cattle. Then check the herd. Get a head count and look for any injured or weak animals and calves. I think we had a few catch pregnant before we brought the bulls down. The rest of us won't be far behind."

Once Ty and Luke were on their way, Wyatt returned to the camp. Teddie was up and sitting next to Hank, sipping from a metal camping mug. He tapped her gently on the shoulder as he passed her, then he grabbed a cup and poured himself some coffee.

An hour later, everyone was on their horses headed up the mountain, while Hank stayed at the campsite to clean up. Teddie was right up front and ready to help. To Wyatt's surprise, she fit right in with the ranch hands, laughing and joking with them, eager to make friends. It was more than her father had ever done. Everett didn't even know any of their names.

She was good with a horse, too, not that he was surprised. Teddie grew up on the ranch and had been riding horses since she was a little girl. He wasn't remotely worried about her helping to bring the cattle down, because he knew she'd follow directions and work just as hard as everyone else. He'd always admired her work ethic.

Two-thirds of the way up the mountain was an alpine meadow, stretching out like a lush, green quilt dotted with purple and blue wildflowers. The smell of sweet clover and damp earth mixed with the overwhelming odor of the evergreen pines surrounding the meadow. The cattle moved as one, shifting restlessly and staring uneasily at the border collies.

Wyatt adjusted the grip on his reins and turned his horse to face the others. "We need to keep them tight," he said, eyes scanning the herd. "No stragglers. Let's move 'em out."

The ranch hands fanned out, pressing the herd together. Luke whistled, and the dogs moved as one, helping them push the cattle in the direction they wanted them to move. The animals' hooves churned up dust, while the occasional snort or sharp bark broke the mountain's silence.

Wyatt kept one eye on Teddie, who was off to the side, monitoring some of the more skittish cattle. Jesse and one of his ranch hands, Clay, followed Teddie to make sure no cattle lagged behind.

Wyatt led the way, keeping a steady pace. The descent down the mountain was slow work. Some cattle had a difficult time with the steeper parts, hesitating on the loose rocks. They moved slowly, keeping the herd safe from injury.

When they were a little more than halfway down, they reached a narrow pass, forcing them to slow down and push the cattle through three or four at a time. It was tough going; the cows were hesitant, snorting and agitated. Wyatt and the others guided them through carefully, talking low and steady until they were through the pass. The dogs and Teddie rounded up the few stragglers, returning them to the herd.

After they made it through, the land evened out, and the pace picked up. The cattle moved quickly, as if they knew the open pastures of Cherry Ridge were waiting for them. The tension eased in Wyatt's chest. They were almost home. Two or three more hours, and this would be over.

Moving the cattle stressed him out, especially in the heat of the day. Things had gone far smoother than he'd expected. They'd stopped frequently for water breaks alongside the creek that flowed down the hill, which helped keep the animals hydrated.

Wyatt dropped back until he was keeping pace with Teddie. "Not bad, Calloway."

Teddie laughed and smiled. "You're not half bad yourself, Mr. Dawson."

"I do my best, ma'am," he whispered. "You know, I love Cherry Ridge as much as you do. I've been working on this ranch for half my life. I don't want to see it sold any more than you do."

"Don't worry," she replied. "I'm not giving up that easy. Cherry Ridge is my legacy, and I will not let it go. I'll figure something out. Nobody is taking this place away from me, not even my father."

Wyatt knew she meant it. He just hoped she didn't get hurt.

—

He parked behind the stable, grabbed his coffee, and climbed out of his truck. Wyatt scrubbed a hand over his face and hurried inside. There wasn't enough caffeine in the world to combat his exhaustion.

Working the ranch meant he didn't get days off. After bringing the cattle down the mountain and getting them to pasture, he and the other ranch hands had worked late into the night, checking for any animals that might have suffered wounds and counting the new babies that had been born while they were on the mountain. It looked like they'd lost about five, but they'd gained at least ten babies, maybe more. He'd planned on going back out today, but Hank had brought him the bad news that the truck was giving him trouble. He'd barely made it back to the ranch.

Wyatt hadn't wanted to waste any time, so he stayed until almost midnight working on the truck. He discovered cracked fuel lines and a corroded, leaking tank. Unfortunately, he'd been so damn tired he couldn't keep his eyes open. He headed home, deciding to fix everything in the morning.

He fed the horses, then he checked to see if there were any pressing issues he needed to deal with before he worked on the truck. After he called Hank to send him to town for parts, he poured himself another cup of coffee and headed outside.

He set to work, tearing it apart to replace the worn-out parts with new ones. The temperature spiked as the sun rose, its angry rays beating down on him, adding to his exhaustion. Sweat rolled down Wyatt's neck and along his spine, settling in the middle of his back, staining his shirt.

It took him almost two hours to change everything out, and he made a mess, spilling gas on the ground beneath the truck. As soon as he got it out of the way, he'd soak up what he could with the bag of cat litter they kept in the garage, clean it up, and run it down to Kane's auto shop so he could dispose of it properly.

Wyatt started the truck, satisfied that he'd fixed the gas leak, pushed open the door, and jumped out. He stretched, groaning as the muscles in his back, shoulders, and legs screamed in protest. He was in good shape, but everybody had a limit, and he had just about reached his.

"Did you get that beast running?"

He looked up to see Jesse walking his way. He raised a hand and nodded, frowning when he noticed Preston strolling behind Jesse like he owned the place.

Jesse got to him first. "Sorry about this, but he insisted on tagging along, said he needs to talk to the Colonel. I don't know why he's following me down here. I told him Calloway is probably in the house."

Wyatt sighed and braced himself. He had never gotten along with Preston Remington. He was three years younger—the same age as Teddie—and they hadn't run in the same circles in high school. Preston came from money while Wyatt had been working since he was a kid. They weren't friends, and frankly, Preston annoyed him.

"Hot out today, isn't it?" Preston said when he reached them.

Wyatt rolled his eyes. Preston had just stepped out of an air-conditioned vehicle and there wasn't a drop of sweat on him. He didn't know what an honest day's work was. The man had done nothing more strenuous than raise a cigarette to his mouth.

"What are you doing here, Preston?" he asked.

Preston scowled. "I'm meeting with the Colonel. I have an offer for the ranch."

"Is Teddie involved in those discussions?"

"Why would she be involved?" Preston scoffed.

Wyatt sighed. "Teddie runs this place. She needs to be a part of any discussions you have about *anything* to do with Cherry Ridge."

Preston shook his head. "If her father wants her involved, he'll let me know."

"I don't think she'll like that," Wyatt countered.

"I don't care." Preston shrugged. He flicked his lit cigarette at Wyatt, whose eyes followed it as it arched, the glowing ember of red and orange tumbling through the air.

His shout of "What are you doing?" caught in his throat.

The cigarette bounced on the hard-packed dirt and rolled under the truck, right into the gas that had leaked from the busted fuel lines. Time stopped, and for a heartbeat, there was nothing. Wyatt turned, foolishly thinking he could stop what was about to happen. The gasoline caught the flame and then there was a loud whooshing sound, then—BOOM!

It was deafening, like a crack of thunder as it struck a tree. A thunderous shockwave tore through the ranch, rattling windows and sending a fiery plume shooting into the sky. The force of the explosion lifted the truck off the ground, shattering the windshield as the metal shell of the vehicle crumpled in on itself like paper.

Wyatt's eardrums exploded, and an immediate ringing filled his head as bright, hot, orange light blinded him and unbelievable, intense heat surrounded him. The world tilted on its axis as hell rained down.

Chapter 9
Teddie

Teddie was at her desk, head resting on her folded arms, half asleep, when the explosion rocked the guest house, rattling the windows and shaking the furniture. The shock made her fall out of her chair and hit the floor.

"What the hell?" she muttered, pushing herself to her feet.

She raced for the door, leaving it wide open as she burst through it and darted around the side of the house.

A hundred yards from the barn, before she had even emerged from the orchard, Teddie slid to a stop, frozen in place as she watched thick, black smoke rise into the sky. Shouts echoed in the chaos as men cursed and coughed, scrambling to get to their feet. An unrecognizable pile of burning metal sat in the middle of the gravel drive, flames popping and crackling, the heat so intense she felt it where she stood.

"Oh my god," she moaned, fear turning her blood to ice.

Horses neighed and kicked at their stall doors as the fire licked at the sides of the barn. The air was thick with smoke and panic as people ran around yelling, screaming, and crying.

"Ms. Calloway!" Luke yelled, running toward her. "What the hell happened?"

"I don't know." The need to panic built in her chest, but she pushed it down. She had to keep it together, take care of the ranch. "Luke, grab Jed and check on the horses. If they need to be moved out of the barn, take them to the pens north of the barn. Tell Hank, Ty, and Nash to get the hoses and put this fire out. Now."

"Yes, ma'am." He turned to go, but Teddie grabbed his arm.

"Where's Wyatt?"

Luke swallowed and shook his head. "I haven't seen him."

She nodded. "Okay. Go! Go!"

Luke took off at a dead run.

"Wyatt!" Teddie screamed, looking everywhere at once.

Hand up in front of her face in a futile effort to keep the heat from licking at her skin, she circled the burning hunk of metal—what she suspected was the ranch truck, the one that constantly broke down. On the far side of the tractor, on his stomach, was a man covered in soot.

Teddie fell to her knees beside him and rolled him over, but it wasn't Wyatt, it was Jesse. His eyes rolled back in his head, deep coughs left him, and blood poured from his ears. She sagged in relief, but the fear was still there.

She pulled Jesse's head into her lap and called for help. Maggie appeared at her side a few seconds later.

"I got him, sweetheart," her mother said. "Where's Wyatt?"

"I don't know."

"Go find him," Maggie instructed.

Teddie nodded as she got to her feet, the tears threatening to fall. She held them off by sheer force of will as she turned in circles, desperately looking for Wyatt. She ducked around the people with buckets and hoses who worked to douse the flames before they reached the barn and the horses.

That was when she saw him lying motionless near the stable wall, half buried under a pile of hay, a large bleeding gash above his left eyebrow, and various other cuts and bruises covered every inch of visible skin.

"Wyatt!" Teddie ran to his side, dropping to her knees beside him as tears poured down her face.

He stirred, a deep groan leaving him. He grabbed her hand. "Hey, it's okay," he murmured. "I'm okay."

"Jesus Christ, no you're not! You're bleeding! I... I thought you were dead. I couldn't find you, and when I saw Jesse, I thought it was you—" She sobbed, the tears blurring her vision.

"I'm sorry," he mumbled.

Only Wyatt thought to apologize for almost dying. He had to be the most selfless, amazing man she'd ever met. "If you had died, I'd have killed you myself."

He chuckled and shook his head, but the laugh quickly changed to a groan. He furrowed his brow, narrowed his eyes, pressed his lips tight together, and hunched his shoulders.

"You're not okay," she said.

"I'm not okay," he replied just before he passed out.

—

Sleep was elusive, not that she could have slept with Wyatt lying unconscious in his hospital bed, every wire imaginable attached to him. Teddie checked to make sure he was still asleep before she slipped out of his room in the ICU and headed down the hall to the vending machines. She didn't want to be gone too long; Wyatt was in and out of consciousness, and she wanted to be there if he woke up again.

The concussion he'd suffered was severe, along with a burst eardrum, multiple lacerations, and several burns. When the truck exploded, the blast threw him over ten feet, where he thankfully landed in a pile of hay bales next to the barn before he blacked out.

Jesse was in a room down the hall, but unlike Wyatt, he hadn't regained consciousness. His wife, Claire, had not left his side. They had crossed paths several times, meeting at the vending machines or the nurses' station. Teddie's heart broke for her. The doctors didn't have any answers; they weren't sure Jesse would wake up, and if he did, what condition he would be in.

"Theodora."

Her shoulders slumped at the sound of her father's voice. She'd avoided her father ever since Wyatt ended up in the hospital, refusing to speak to him. She slowly turned around, crossing her arms over her chest as she stared at him.

"Colonel," she said.

"How long has this been going on?" he asked.

Teddie sighed. "How long has *what* been going on?" she retorted, knowing full well what he was talking about, but still playing dumb.

Everett grabbed her arm and dragged her into the waiting area, away from the nurses' station. He dropped her arm and turned to glare at her. "Do not play dumb with me, young lady. You know *exactly* what I'm talking about. You and that ranch hand."

"Wyatt Dawson, your ranch *foreman*?"

Her father rolled his eyes. "Fine. How long have you and Dawson been together?"

She gritted her teeth. "I don't know. A while. A few months." It had been much longer than that, but she wasn't ready to tell him that.

"You know my rule—"

"Your archaic rule about the staff not mingling with your daughters? That rule? I am aware of it."

"You need to end it."

Teddie shook her head. "Absolutely not."

"I am not giving you an option," her father said. "End it."

His phone rang before she could reply. He yanked it out of his suit jacket and looked at it. "It's the insurance company." He gave her one of his "this isn't over" looks, turned away from her, and answered the phone. Teddie stared at his back for a minute before she walked away and returned to Wyatt's room.

According to the doctor, he was still in and out of consciousness, so she picked up her book and sat in the chair next to his bed to wait for him to wake up. Not that she read much, just stared at the pages, basically sleeping with her eyes open. She didn't know what time it was when

Wyatt whispered her name. She got up so fast her book hit the floor.

"Hi," she breathed, falling to her knees beside the bed.

"Hey," he mumbled.

Teddie fought back tears of relief and pushed down her emotions, doing her best to keep herself calm. She took his face in her hands and kissed him, brushing a thumb over the bruise on the side of his face.

"Don't cry," he said, grabbing her hand and squeezing it. "I'm alive."

Teddie nodded and wiped the tears from her cheeks. She grabbed the chair, pulled up to the bed, and sat down with her feet tucked beneath her. She held Wyatt's hand and spent the next hour answering his questions—how the horses were, how much damage the buildings had sustained, who else had been hurt, and anything he wanted to know. When he finished asking questions, it was her turn.

"What the hell happened?"

Wyatt told her what he remembered, which was only until the truck exploded. By the time he finished, he had trouble keeping his eyes open. He dozed off with his hand in hers.

—

Later that day, the nurses, with Wyatt's help, convinced her to go home for a few hours to shower, sleep, and get some proper food in her body. They assured her that if anything changed, she would be the first person they called. Teddie reluctantly agreed.

Tessa greeted her at the door with a hug, holding her tighter than she ever had before. Then she took her sister's hand and led her to the dining room, where she had a plate of food and a cold bottle of beer waiting for her.

"You should have told me," Tessa scolded. "About you and Wyatt."

"I didn't tell anybody," Teddie replied. "I didn't want anybody to know."

"Because of the Colonel?"

Teddie nodded, her stomach churning at the mere mention of her father. She would have to face him again eventually, something she was not looking forward to. In fact, she dreaded it. She pushed the thought aside while she ate the sandwich and drank her beer, even though she had little appetite.

"Did you know he was going to go to the hospital?" Teddie asked between bites of food.

Tessa nodded. "On his way out the door, he quizzed me, wondering if I knew you were dating 'that ranch hand.' When I said no, he told me it didn't matter, because he was going to put an end to it. I wanted to stop him. That's a fight I do not *want* to relive."

Teddie shook her head. "You didn't have to do that."

"Yes, I did." Tessa exhaled loudly. "Not that it mattered."

Teddie had finished eating when the kitchen door slammed.

"Tessa!" their father roared. "Where is your sister?"

"Did he sound like that when you were fighting?" Teddie mumbled.

"Yep. Exactly like that," Tessa replied.

Teddie swallowed half the bottle of beer, handed it to her sister, and wiped her mouth with the back of her hand. She stood up and braced herself.

"I'm in the dining room, Daddy!" she yelled. She pointed at the door on the other side of the room that led to a back hallway and mouthed, "Go."

For once, Tessa didn't argue with her. Instead, she got up and walked away, shaking her head and mumbling under her breath.

Everett Calloway strode through the door a minute later with his fists clenched and his brow furrowed, looking as if he was about to erupt in hellfire. Teddie sucked in a deep breath and braced herself for a tongue lashing.

He stopped in front of her, arms crossed, his face unreadable. "Well?"

"Well, what?"

"Did you end your relationship with Dawson?" he asked.

Teddie rubbed her forehead. "Do you realize you have not *once* asked how he is? He was injured in an accident on *our* ranch, and the only thing you care about is whether or not he is dating your daughter. He is tired and in pain, but instead of worrying about healing, he is worried you're going to fire him."

"Which is exactly what I'm going to do," Everett stated.

She could barely contain her anger, the need to lash out at her father overwhelming her. "Why, Daddy? Because he broke your archaic rule about dating one of the Calloway girls?"

"Not only that. He almost cost us everything. We were lucky to put the fire out before it reached the stables. The truck exploded, a truck he'd been working on—"

"It wasn't his fault," Teddie interjected. "Preston Remington dropped his cigarette."

Everett rolled his eyes. "I don't want to hear any excuses. Preston explained what happened, and it sounds like Dawson didn't clean up the gasoline, which ignited the fire. It wasn't Preston's fault."

"Jesus Christ, Daddy—"

"Do not swear at me, Theodora," he snapped.

"I cannot believe you are going to blame this on Wyatt." She sucked in a deep breath. "You're going to fire him because of what Preston did?"

"He blew up the ranch truck and almost killed my horses!"

"No. Preston did that by carelessly dropping a still-lit cigarette on the ground. But you are so dead set on this being the fault of the ranch hand dating your daughter that you refuse to accept the truth. You want a legitimate excuse to fire him, so you're grabbing onto this. You are so damn thick!"

The anger radiating from her father forced her back a step. "This discussion is over, Theodora. I am firing Dawson, and you *will* stop seeing him. Period." He turned to leave.

"You can't tell me what to do," she argued. "I am a grown woman."

"You live under my roof and you work for me, so yes, I *can* tell you what to do." He stormed out of the room.

"Not if I don't live under your roof," she muttered.

Chapter 10

Teddie

*T*eddie yanked open her dresser drawers, tossed her suitcases on the bed, and randomly threw stuff in them. She wasn't paying attention to what she grabbed—she didn't care—she wanted to pack so she could get out of the house. Once both of the suitcases were full, she picked up a duffle bag, took it into the bathroom, and threw her toiletries in it.

Fifteen minutes later, she had everything loaded in her Jeep, and she was on her way down the drive, heading for Wyatt's. He lived in a small cabin on the north end of the property, about five minutes from the house.

Under the mat in front of the door, she found Wyatt's extra key and unlocked the front door. She got her things from the car and went inside, locking the door behind her and dropping the key in a little glass bowl on the table. Teddie sat on the couch and stared off into space.

This shit flipped her life upside down. Her father was going to sell the ranch—the only home she'd ever known—and the man she loved was in the hospital. Everything was out of control.

"Maybe not everything," she muttered. She grabbed her laptop out of her backpack and opened it.

There had to be a way to save the ranch without selling it to the Remingtons—a loan or an investor. If she figured something out, some way to buy the ranch from her father, she and Wyatt could run it together.

Exhaustion washed over her, so she kicked off her boots and stretched out on the couch, a small throw pillow under her head. Within minutes, she was sound asleep.

Teddie was still at Wyatt's place when he came home from the hospital. Of course, he told her she was welcome to stay as long as she liked, even it meant forever. She wondered if he was joking, though she didn't think he was.

"What did Claire say?" she asked after Wyatt hung up his phone. "How is Jesse?"

"He's angry, hurt, pissed, and out for blood," Wyatt said. "Anybody would be after losing their hearing in one ear in an accident that never should have happened." He eased onto the couch beside Teddie and slipped his arm around her shoulder.

"How are you doing?" he asked.

"I'm fine," she replied, a little too quickly.

"Liar," he whispered, kissing her cheek. "It's been almost a week since the fight with your father. Are you going to call him?"

"No," she snapped.

"Hey, hey, easy. It was only a suggestion."

Teddie sighed, turning in his arms to lay her head on his chest. Wyatt kissed the top of her head and rubbed circles on her back.

She felt bad that he was comforting her because he'd only been out of the hospital for three days. The severe concussion he suffered was causing him debilitating migraines, and he still lived with the prospect of being fired.

"I'm sorry I snapped at you," she murmured. "All of this stuff with the ranch is putting me on edge. Every day I am not there is a day when my father might sell it right out from under me."

"What time is your meeting with the bank tomorrow?"

"Nine a.m. I'm nervous about it, though. I have nothing of my own to prove I can repay a loan large enough to purchase Cherry Ridge. I don't even own my Jeep, for Christ's sake. My father bought it for me. I have a few credit cards in my name, but shit, do I even have a job anymore? I work for the Colonel, and I walked out." Teddie abruptly stood up and paced. "I'm not sure I can do this, Wyatt. Am I capable of running the ranch by myself?"

"Honey, you run it by yourself now. What exactly does your father do?"

Teddie took a deep breath, prepared to spout off a list of everything her father did, and then froze. Nothing came to mind. She was in charge of the financial aspects of the ranch, management of the land, servicing the equipment and structures on the ranch, most of their business relationships, and the buying and selling of the cattle. About the only thing she didn't do was hire the staff, though she took care of the payroll and their employment records. They knew if they needed anything, they should come to her.

"I... I guess I run Cherry Ridge, don't I?"

Wyatt leaned forward with his elbows on his knees. "You are the one with the connections, right?"

She snorted. "Are you reading my mind? I was just thinking that."

"Well, are you?"

Teddie nodded. "Yeah, I am."

"You need to use those relationships, babe. You have the connections; people come to you when they want to work with Cherry Ridge. Reach out. See if you can scare up some investors or a co-signer on the loan to buy the ranch."

"I don't know—"

Wyatt shook his head. "No, that's not an answer. If you want to keep this place, your childhood home, then you don't have much choice. Put together a proposal and start asking around."

Jesus, he was right. This ranch was hers. She understood it better than anyone in her family. If her father wasn't willing to let her have it, then she'd buy it out from underneath him.

"Have told you I love you yet today?" she asked.

He smirked. "Only four or five times."

"Will you come to the bank with me?"

"I can't," Wyatt replied. "I'm meeting with the insurance inspector tomorrow."

"That's tomorrow? What time?"

"I think around eleven," he said.

"I'll be there. I'll be done at the bank by then, so I can meet you at the insurance office."

He reached for her hand, tugging her close. "You don't have to do that. I can go on my own."

"I'm not letting you face Everett Calloway alone. You and me together, right?"

"Yes."

Teddie kneeled on the couch beside him, ran her fingers through his hair, and kissed him.

"How's your head?" she asked.

He shrugged. "Okay. Why?"

"Let's go to bed," she whispered. "You look tired."

"Okay, but I'm gonna shower first."

She kissed him again. "I'm going to clean the kitchen really fast, then I'll be in."

When Teddie walked into the bedroom, Wyatt lay sprawled across the bed, wearing only a towel around his waist. She thought he was asleep until he held his hand out to her and gestured for her to join him.

She stripped off her T-shirt and jeans, eased onto the bed beside him, and let him wrap her in his arms. He rolled to his side, caught her lips in his, and kissed her, a deep, probing kiss that made her toes curl. He slipped his hand into her hair, cupping her head and holding her close as the kiss deepened. Their legs tangled together as Teddie pulled the towel away from his waist and ran her hands over his naked body. She moaned when his hard cock brushed against her leg. She reached for him, her nails grazing the tip of his length, drawing an answering moan from him.

"Is this okay?" she murmured against his lips as she wrapped her hand around his shaft, sliding it down the length, her thumb teasing the tip.

A growl rumbled through his chest. "I'm good, baby." He pushed her hair off her neck, kissing it hungrily.

Teddie pushed him to his back, kissing a trail down his neck and over his chest. Her tongue darted out, swiping at his nipple, circling it. She continued down his stomach, taking her time, enjoying his small gasps and moans, his cock so hard it throbbed in her hand.

She took him in her mouth, her tongue tracing the slit, a shuddering moan escaping her as the velvety soft skin slid past her lips. Teddie wrapped her hand around the base, opened her mouth, and slowly slid it down the shaft, rubbing it against the roof of her mouth.

"Fuck," Wyatt groaned, his hands tangling in her hair as his hips rose off the bed, pushing himself deeper into her mouth.

Teddie hollowed her cheeks and sucked gently, cupping and fondling his sensitive sac as she pulled him deeper into the wet heat of her mouth. She moved back up the length, grazing him with her teeth before repeating the movement several times, each time taking more of his cock, opening her throat to accept his tight, controlled thrusts.

She climbed to her knees, adjusting her position so she hovered over Wyatt, the new angle allowing her to swallow him completely, caressing his sac as he fucked her mouth.

"Jesus, babe, I'm gonna cum." His hands fell to his sides, clutching desperately at the blankets on the bed.

Teddie wrapped her hand around the base of his cock and squeezed, releasing him to look into his lust blown eyes.

"Then do it," she challenged, stroking his length several times before she took him back into her mouth, sliding him past her swollen, saliva-slick lips, her head bobbing as she pleasured him.

A low groan echoed through Wyatt's chest as his cock pulsed in her mouth and his balls drew up tight in her hand, which were the all-too-familiar signs he was about to cum. Teddie intensified her movements, deep-throating him, swallowing him down, the pressure of her constricting throat increasing his pleasure.

Wyatt trembled beneath her, his release accompanied by an obscene moan, his cock jerking as he came, his taste flooding her mouth. She moaned with him, her nose pressed against his curls, taking what he gave her, draining him dry.

When it was over, Wyatt's soft cock slid from her mouth, and she slowly kissed her way up his body. She stretched out on top of him, nuzzling her face into the space where his neck and shoulder met, inhaling the clean scent of his skin.

His fingers drifted lazily up and down her back, his breathing steady and even. Tears welled at the corners of her eyes, the fear she'd held at bay for days threatening to push itself to the surface. Teddie knew she should be relieved life hadn't thrown her a vicious curve ball and stolen Wyatt from her too soon, and she was relieved, but now and then, it snuck up on her, especially in a moment like this.

She pushed herself closer to Wyatt, though it was impossible—they were already skin to skin, limbs tangled together—but that didn't stop her from trying. She held back a terrified sob, not wanting him to know how close she was to losing it.

But he knew; he always did. That was why she loved him. His arms circled her waist, and he rolled them over, the two of them chest to chest. He kissed her, then he tucked her head under his chin.

"I'm right here, baby," he whispered. "I'm right here and I'm not going anywhere. I promise."

Chapter 11
Wyatt

"Mr. Dawson, thank you for meeting me," Lloyd Adams said.

The insurance company had assigned Lloyd to investigate the explosion and subsequent fire. This was the second time he and Wyatt had met; the first time had been while he was in the hospital, twenty-four hours after the fire, when he'd been less than coherent.

A sharp rap at the door drew Lloyd's attention. He excused himself, went to his office door, and stepped outside. Thirty seconds later, Teddie blew through the door, obviously irritated, with Lloyd right behind her, and took a seat beside Wyatt.

"Um, Ms. Calloway, it's... I don't think... it's not a good idea for you to be here," Lloyd stammered. "I'll speak with you after the investigation."

Teddie shook her head. "Thank you, Mr. Adams, but I'd like to sit in on this interview, if you don't mind."

"Well, your father—"

"Has entrusted me with managing Cherry Ridge," she interjected. "That hasn't changed." She looked around the room. "Speaking of my father, where is he?"

Lloyd cleared his throat, took his seat, and shuffled some papers around. "I, uh, I thought Colonel Calloway was going to be in attendance, but it looks like he won't make it." He cleared his throat again. "Mr. Dawson, can you tell me about Preston Remington?"

Wyatt sat up straight, surprised that Preston's name had come up. When he'd told Lloyd about Preston and his cigarette when he saw him at the hospital, Lloyd kept bringing the conversation back around to Wyatt. He'd subtly hinted that because Wyatt had been fixing the truck prior to the explosion, it was his fault.

"Preston Remington?" Wyatt asked.

"Yes, sir," Lloyd replied.

Wyatt sighed. "Like I said before, Preston threw a lit cigarette, which landed in a puddle of gasoline under the truck that I was repairing. That caused the explosion and fire." He shifted in his seat. "Why are you asking?"

"I've talked to almost everyone working that day, and they all said that while Mr. Remington was on site, he was not working. Is that true?"

"Yes," Teddie answered. "Mr. Remington doesn't work for Cherry Ridge. I believe he was there to meet with my father."

Lloyd nodded and scribbled something on a notepad. "Okay, several of them also mentioned they believe Mr. Remington is a chain smoker, so it is possible the story you told me—"

"It's not a story, Mr. Adams," Wyatt snapped. "It's the truth."

"And that's what I'm trying to get to. The truth." Lloyd held his pen over the paper on his desk. "Tell me again what happened."

Wyatt went through it again, every second, from the minute he finished working on the truck to waking up in the hospital. He explained that he'd parked the truck in front of the barn, noticed it leaking gasoline, and hadn't cleaned up thoroughly before Preston arrived. He told Lloyd about Preston carelessly tossing his lit cigarette toward the truck and how he had tried to stop it, knowing full well he couldn't. Then he explained his vague memories of the explosion, the fire, and his pain. By the time he finished, he was sweating profusely.

Lloyd nodded and scribbled something on the papers on his desk. "Thank you, Mr. Dawson. I appreciate your help." He got to his feet, shook their hands, and escorted them to the door.

Wyatt took Teddie's hand as they walked out. They were almost out of the building when someone called her name. They turned to see Preston striding purposefully toward them.

"Teddie, wait!"

"Keep walking," he muttered.

"No," Teddie replied. "If I don't talk to him, he'll keep following us and yelling."

"Preston," she said when he slid to a stop in front of them. "What are you doing here?"

"That insurance guy wants to talk to me." He shrugged and turned to Wyatt, smirking. "He probably needs my help to get Wyatt fired for setting your ranch on fire."

Teddie must have seen the look on Wyatt's face because she stepped between them. "Knock it off, Preston. We know whose fault it was that the truck exploded. Stop acting like you didn't do anything wrong."

"I dropped a cigarette, Teddie. I didn't set off a goddamn bomb."

Lloyd cleared his throat from behind them. "Excuse me, Mr. Remington. I'm ready to see you now."

Preston grumbled something incoherent, then he followed Lloyd into his office.

—

Wyatt slid into the booth across from Teddie, took off his hat, and put it on the seat beside him. He ordered a cup of coffee for himself and an iced tea for Teddie. When she returned from the bathroom, she kissed him on the cheek and sat down.

"I didn't get a chance to ask you yet. How did it go at the bank?" he said.

She sipped her drink, then set it down with a sigh. "Okay, I guess."

"That doesn't sound good."

"Well, they're willing to help me get the money for the ranch," she replied.

"Why do I sense a 'but' coming?"

"*But* they want a co-signer or an investor to sign off on it." She shrugged. "Who the hell am I going to ask? Anybody I ask will want a say in how to run the ranch, and I don't think I'm okay with that. I'm not sure what to do."

Wyatt reached across the table and took her hand. "Can I ask you a question?"

"Yeah, of course."

"If Cherry Ridge were gone, if your father sells it, what would you do? Where would you go?"

Teddie opened her mouth, then she snapped it shut and shook her head. "I... I don't know."

He squeezed her hand. "Then that answers your question. If you can't see yourself anywhere else or doing anything else, that means Cherry Ridge is where you're meant to be."

"But my father—"

Wyatt slammed his fist on the table, making her jump. "Damn your father. He didn't care about you when he decided to sell the ranch, did he? So, why should you care about him? Stop tiptoeing around what the Colonel wants and decide what you want. And *who* you want."

Teddie yanked her hand out of his and sat back. "What is that supposed to mean?"

He rubbed his forehead. "Look, babe, I know you love me. I do. But you are still afraid of upsetting your father."

"That's not true," she argued.

Wyatt held up his hand. "You've been staying with me for almost a week, right? Have you unpacked anything? Picked up the rest of your stuff from the main house? No. Because you're just biding your time until you can move back home."

"It's my *home*, Wyatt."

He sighed and rubbed his head. "I know. The question is, do you want it to be *our* home?"

"What?"

"Do you see us running Cherry Ridge together?" he asked, though he thought he knew the answer.

"I... I don't know," she whispered. "I won't lie. I have thought about it."

"Do you see us running it together as partners, or do you see yourself as the owner and me as your foreman? As your employee?" he asked.

Teddie opened her mouth, then snapped it shut. That was all the answer he needed.

"I don't know," she repeated.

"I was afraid you were going to say that." Wyatt pulled a box out of his pocket, opened it, and set it on the table. "I've been carrying this around in my pocket for more than a month, waiting for the right moment, waiting until you were ready to tell your father about us." He shook his head and stared at a spot above her head. "When you told me you loved me on the mountain, I thought our moment had come, but then you said you weren't ready to tell your father. Tell me, have you told the Colonel you love me, or does he think we're just dating?"

Teddie swallowed, her eyes glued to the diamond and sapphire ring in the box. Tears welled in her eyes.

"Answer me, Teddie. Have you told the Colonel you love me?"

She slowly shook her head. "No, I haven't told him I love you. Not yet."

"When are you planning on doing that?" he asked.

"Wyatt," she whispered.

"So, you haven't told your father you're in love with me, and you still see me as your employee, not your equal? Do I have it right?"

"You're not being fair. I'm under a lot of stress right now." She gnawed on her bottom lip. "I don't want to add to it."

He nodded, his fingers tapping on the table, then he picked up the box with the engagement ring and shoved it in his pocket. "You know what? I'm gonna head home. I'm kind of tired, and I think a headache is coming on." He took out his wallet, dropped some money on the table, and then he stood up. "I'll see you later."

"Wyatt, wait," Teddie pleaded.

He stopped and looked at her over his shoulder. "I'd co-sign that loan for you, by the way. In a heartbeat. I've been saving every dime I've earned since I was sixteen, hoping someday I could buy a ranch of my own. It would be a dream come true if I could even be a part-owner of Cherry Ridge. I love that place almost as much as you love it. Hell, I love it almost as much as I love you. Nothing would be better than owning it with the woman I want to marry."

Teddie stared at him with tears sliding down her cheeks, but she didn't speak. Wyatt turned and left. It was up to her now. It was her decision to make.

Chapter 12
Teddie

She watched him walk away. She sat on her ass as the man she loved walked away and she didn't stop him.

Teddie wiped the tears from her face and finished her drink. Then she left, waving goodbye to the bar's owner, Nate, and his fiancée, Faith, on her way out. She climbed in her Jeep and stared out the window at Flathead Lake for almost half an hour, figuring out what she wanted to do—go home and have it out with her father or go apologize to Wyatt. She was still deciding what to do when her cell phone buzzed with an incoming message.

[Everett: I need to talk to you.]

Sighing, she quickly typed a response, then started the Jeep. She glanced at the phone she'd tossed on the passenger seat.

[Teddie: On my way.]

[Everett: Meet me in the office.]

It took her almost twenty minutes to drive to Cherry Ridge. As soon as she drove up the driveway, her mother came out of the house and waited for her at the top of the curve. She was barely out of the Jeep before Maggie descended on her and wrapped her in a hug.

"I've missed you," she whispered.

"I missed you, too, Mom."

Maggie held her at arm's length. "Where have you been staying?"

Teddie cleared her throat. "With Wyatt."

"Good, he needs someone to take care of him," her mother said. "How is he?"

"On the mend," Teddie replied. "Mom, did you know about me and Wyatt?"

Maggie shrugged. "I suspected the two of you were seeing each other, but I didn't want to interfere. I knew you'd tell me when you were ready."

"Did you tell Daddy?"

Her mother shook her head. "It's not my place to tell him. He needed to hear it from you, especially if you have feelings for Wyatt. Do you?"

"Yes, I do. I'm, well, I'm pretty sure I'm in love with him."

Maggie's smile widened. "I knew it!" She slapped a hand over her mouth. "Sorry," she mumbled through her fingers. "I'm happy that you found somebody to love."

"Thanks, Mom." Teddie took a deep breath. "Is Daddy in the guesthouse? He summoned me."

Her mother nodded. "He's waiting for you. Go easy on him."

Teddie laughed. "Excuse me? *Me* go easy on *him*?"

"Don't worry, I said the same thing to your father." Maggie hugged her again. "Come see me before you leave. I have a cherry pie for Wyatt." She turned and went back into her kitchen.

Next up was Tessa, who jumped on Teddie—literally—from the porch. Tessa wrapped her arms around her sister and held her so tight she couldn't breathe.

"Thanks for leaving me alone with the tyrant," Tessa said. "He's been intolerable since you left."

"Shit," Teddie muttered. "Seriously?"

Tessa rolled her eyes. "Okay, maybe not completely intolerable, but difficult. I've been hiding out with Mom in her kitchen."

"Did he tell you what he's going to do?" Teddie asked.

"What do you mean? What is he going to do?"

"Sell Cherry Ridge," Teddie replied.

"Holy shit, what? He's going to sell the ranch? Can he... can he do that?"

"It's his ranch, Tess. He owns it, so he has the right to do whatever he wants."

Her sister crossed her arms and shot a dirty look over her shoulder at the guesthouse. "So, where does that leave us?"

Teddie grinned. "Homeless?"

"Ha-ha, you're funny. I'm being serious."

"So am I. And I don't know where that leaves us, but I'm going to find out." She patted Tessa's arm. "I promise I'll figure it out. I better go; Daddy is waiting."

"Good luck," Tessa murmured. "You'll need it."

Thanks to her pessimistic family, Teddie's nerves had ratcheted up tenfold. She marched down the sidewalk to the guesthouse, raised her hand to knock, then changed her mind, opened the door, and went inside.

Her father was at her desk, staring at her computer with an angry look on his face. He punched a few buttons on the keyboard, then shoved it away, muttering obscenities under his breath.

"Problem?" she asked.

Everett swung around, his look of anger moving from the computer to her. "It's about time."

"Daddy, you texted me less than thirty minutes ago. I was in town, but after I got your text, I came straight here. What is the problem?"

"I need the ranch's financials for the last year," he said. "But I can't find them, and your computer is password protected."

"Yes, it is," Teddie said. "Why do you need the financials?"

"There is a buyer interested in Cherry Ridge, but he wants to see the financials before he decides." Everett got to his feet. "Can you get them for me?"

"I want to talk to you first."

Her father rolled his eyes. "About what?"

"About Cherry Ridge," she explained. "I'd like to make you a counteroffer."

"What? A counteroffer on the ranch? Are you serious?"

"I'm dead serious, Daddy. I want a chance to buy my childhood home before you sell it out from underneath me. Not only is this place my home, but it's my legacy, my *life*. I have devoted the last eleven years to Cherry Ridge. I know this place inside and out. I want the chance to take it over and make it mine. All mine."

Everett tipped his head to one side and narrowed his eyes. "Well, it certainly sounds like you mean business."

"Yes," she replied. "I do."

Her father slowly nodded his head. "Okay, I'll give you a chance to make an offer. I won't accept anything without letting you make a counteroffer. But I'm only giving you thirty-six hours. Does that sound fair?"

Without thinking about it, Teddie threw her arms around her father and hugged him. To her surprise, he patted her on the back. Everett Calloway wasn't one for affection, so a pat on the back was a big deal.

"Let me know when your counteroffer is ready, and we'll talk." He was almost to the door when he stopped, though he didn't turn around. "Are you planning on moving back home anytime soon?"

"I don't know," she murmured. "Are you still mad that I'm dating Wyatt?"

Everett's shoulders stiffened. "Maybe."

"Then, no, I'm not coming home. Not yet."

"Will you at least come back to work? There's a lot that needs to be done."

"Are you saying you need me?"

Her father sighed. "Theodora, don't test me."

"I'm sorry." She cleared her throat. "I'll be in tomorrow morning, first thing."

He nodded once, then he strode from the room without looking back.

Teddie dropped into the chair at her desk with a sigh. Everett Calloway was exhausting on a good day. She pushed a hand through her hair and got up. She'd say goodbye to her mom and sister, grab some clothes, and go back to Wyatt's. It was time to apologize to him.

—

She reached for the door handle, paused for a second, then instead of opening the door, she knocked. A few minutes later, the door flew open and there stood Wyatt with a strange look on his face.

"Why are you knocking?" he asked.

"I... well, I don't live here. I'm a guest."

Wyatt rolled her eyes, grabbed her arm, and yanked her inside. "Don't be silly. Get in here."

Teddie dropped her bag of clothes on the floor and followed him through the living room to the kitchen.

"You made dinner?" she whispered.

"Chili, cornbread, beer, nothing special. I thought you might be hungry, since you didn't eat breakfast or lunch."

As if on cue, her stomach growled, and Wyatt chuckled. "Sit down and eat."

"You're not mad at me anymore?"

He shook his head. "I wasn't mad at you, Ted. I'm angry with the situation and with the uncertainty of our future, and that you haven't told your father you love me."

"I just need a little time," she said.

"I know, and I'm willing to give it to you. But I won't wait forever. I love you, Theodora Jean Calloway, and I want to marry you. But I won't even think about that until the Colonel knows you're in love with me. Period."

Desperate to lighten the moment, Teddie smiled at him. "Did you just middle name me?"

Wyatt nodded. "I did." Unfortunately, he wasn't laughing.

She exhaled. "I *am* sorry, Wyatt. I know that's not what you want to hear, but I am sorry I haven't told my father. You know how difficult he can be, and with everything going on right now, I need to be careful. Once the ranch is mine, I will talk to him about us. I swear. Until then, please be patient with me."

"Once it's yours? Did you talk to your father about buying the ranch?"

"Yes," Teddie responded. "He agreed to let me make a counteroffer, and I'm going to do it."

"Does that mean you're going to get the loan from the bank?"

"I'm going to try."

Wyatt's eyebrows rose. "Who is going to co-sign for you?"

Teddie shrugged. "I don't know yet." She cleared her throat. "I know you offered, and I really appreciate it, but I'm not sure how my father will feel about that, and I don't want to ask you to do something like that. It's not fair to you. Please give me a chance to figure out what I'm going to do, okay? I need you to trust me."

"I can do that," Wyatt said. "But I need a promise from you?"

"Anything."

"After you decide what to do about the ranch, you'll tell your father about us."

"I promise," she whispered. She leaned over the table and kissed him. "I love you, Wyatt James Dawson."

He chuckled. "Did you just middle name me?"

Chapter 13

Wyatt

Wyatt sucked in a deep breath and scanned the area around the barn before he got out of the truck. The ranch hands did their best to clean up the mess caused by the explosion, but a big black spot remained in front of the barn, and there were scorch marks on the outside wall.

He wasn't just checking out what damage had been done, but he was also looking for the Colonel. Seeing Teddie's father wasn't exactly high on his list. In fact, he wasn't even sure if he should be there. The man had threatened to fire him.

"Oh, well," he muttered, pushing open the truck door and stepping out. "Here goes nothing."

Wyatt slammed the door and headed for the barn, skirting the black spot on the ground. He checked on the horses first, then he went to his office. Someone had straightened up his desk and cleaned the bathroom. He chuckled to himself and took a seat behind the desk. It was nice to have people who took care of him.

Once he caught up with what little paperwork he had to finish—mostly payroll stuff—he planned to check on the horses, take the ranch Jeep out to pasture to look over the cattle, and see if Mrs. Calloway needed any help with her cherries. It had been a few weeks since the harvest, and he hadn't checked in with her. He was usually a lot better about stuff like that, but he'd been distracted.

"Knock, knock."

Wyatt looked up. "Speak of the devil."

Maggie laughed. "You were talking about me?"

"No, but I was thinking about you. Well, you and your cherries. How are things going with the shop?"

"Pretty good. I mean, I've been busy, if that's what you're asking." She stepped into his office, crossed the room, and set a pie on the desk. "Teddie forgot about this yesterday."

Wyatt grinned. "You made me a pie? You know how much I love your pies." He got up, walked around his desk, gave her a one-armed hug, and kissed her cheek. "Thank you."

Maggie patted his cheek. "You're welcome. How are you feeling?"

"Okay," he replied. "I get a little woozy now and then, and I'm still getting headaches, but I'm good."

"You shouldn't be working," she scolded.

"I know, but this place won't run itself." He perched on the edge of his desk, crossed his arms, and looked down at Maggie. "So, you know about me and Teddie?"

Maggie nodded. "Of course I do. I'm not stupid. I knew my daughter had fallen head over heels for someone,

I just didn't know who. After the accident, I was pretty sure it was you."

"And you're okay with it?"

"Yes. Why wouldn't I be? You're a good guy, Wyatt. One of the best. Teddie would be hard-pressed to find someone better."

Wyatt laughed and shook his head. "Can you tell Mr. Calloway that?"

"Trust me, I've tried. Even after more than thirty years together, that man doesn't listen to me." She sighed and gave him a weary smile. "I'll keep trying. Anyway, enjoy the pie. I need to get back to baking."

"Do you need any help?"

"Nope, Tessa is coming down to the kitchen. She's been learning to make all the stuff I make."

"Well, that's a surprise."

"Tell me about it. She loved helping me when she was a little girl, but when she hit thirteen, half her brain leaked out her ears and she became … difficult." Maggie giggled. "Look, I better go."

"I'll walk you out." He walked with her to the barn doors, then they parted ways.

Wyatt walked back through the barn, stopping and checking on each horse. When he was done with that, he grabbed the Jeep keys off the hook by the door. Time to check on the cows.

———

The rain came out of nowhere, as it often did during Montana summers. One minute the sun was shining, the next it was pouring buckets of water. He was soaked by the time he got back to the Jeep from the pasture. Instead of switching to his truck, he drove the Jeep straight to the cabin. When he rounded the corner, he saw Teddie on his rain-soaked front porch. No big surprise, since she had called him about ten times while he was out in the pasture and sent twice as many texts. As soon as he shut off the Jeep, she darted down the steps and raced across the wet grass, stopping in front of him and staring up at him.

"Where the hell have you been?" she demanded. "It's been raining for an hour. I called you."

"I was in the south pasture with the cattle," he explained. "My phone doesn't work out there. What's wrong?"

"You've been out of the hospital for what, not even a week, and you're out in the middle of a rainstorm with the cows? Have you lost your mind?"

"No." He chuckled. "Besides, I'm fine. You don't have to worry about me."

"Yes, I do. Jesus, Wyatt, I worry about you constantly, more so since the explosion. Dammit, don't scare me like that." She pounced on him, her mouth warm and hungry against his. His hands were on her before he could think, one hand cupping her cheek, the other in her wet hair, holding her to him.

Wyatt pulled her closer, flush against his chest, her heart beating in time with his. Teddie gripped his shirt, fisting the fabric and dragging him closer. The kiss deepened until they were both breathing hard.

The rain pounded down around them, drenching them both. Teddie's hair stuck to her face, her clothes plastered to her curves, and he couldn't stop drinking her in, not even as his mouth moved to her jaw, her neck, the raindrops on her skin like a sweet nectar.

Her breath hitched in her throat as she slid her fingers under the hem of his soaked shirt, her warm hands splayed over his stomach, and it burned somewhere deep inside him.

Wyatt gripped her hips tight, grinding against her. He kissed her again.

God, this woman was everything to him.

Teddie moaned, and something inside him snapped. He hauled her into his arms like she weighed nothing, her legs going around his waist, her breath warm against his throat. He turned around and pressed her back against the Jeep.

Wyatt didn't care that they were outside, or about the thunder or the lightning, or the mud on his boots. He wanted her, and when he kissed her again, it was with an ache and a hunger he'd kept buried.

"God, I love you," he murmured when he pulled away.

Teddie didn't say a word. She didn't have to. She knew what kind of hold she had over him. He belonged to her, and they both knew it.

"Inside," she said.

His brain short-circuited.

Wyatt caught her lips in another searing kiss, and he moved, one hand gripping the back of her thigh as he carried her up the porch steps, the other around her waist. His shoulder hit the half-open door, opening it all the way. He stumbled inside, bumping against the doorframe, not that either of them noticed. Teddie kicked the door shut.

He set her on her feet and pressed her back against the wall, not gently, but urgently, nothing left to hold back his desire for her. Their lips met again in a messy, wet, teeth-clashing kiss. Her hand scrambled at the buttons on his shirt, yanking it open and shoving it off his shoulders. Her eyes dropped to his chest, and her breath caught in her throat.

His hands slid under her shirt, skimming her damp skin, up her ribs, and cupped her breasts. She gasped when his fingers brushed against her tight nipples; the sound swallowed by his lips on hers.

Both of their shirts hit the floor, and then there was nothing but mouths, hands, and a delicious friction, her chest against his, both of them slick with rain and flushed.

"Bedroom," he muttered, his voice so low and thick he barely recognized it.

Teddie nodded, her eyes dark and dazed.

Wyatt picked her up again, Teddie laughing into his mouth between kisses as he barreled through the house like a drunk on a bender. Once they got to the bedroom, he dropped her on the bed in the tangled sheets, then he stripped off her soaked denim jeans and underwear. He stared at her, drinking her in before he peeled off his own clothes and joined her on the bed.

He hovered over her, kissing her as one hand skimmed down her side and between her legs. He couldn't wait. He needed her, wanted her more than anything he'd ever wanted in his life. His hunger for her burned deep inside him, insatiable and relentless.

Teddie moaned his name, arching into him when he settled between her legs and pushed into her in one long, slow, aching stroke that had them both trembling with desire.

It wasn't slow or gentle; it was need and instinct, their wet skin sliding against each other. Her hands fisted in his hair, dragging his mouth to her throat, while his grip on her hips left finger-shaped bruises.

They moved together like it was the most perfect union in the world, hell in the universe. Her nails dug into his back, both of them chasing the pleasure. Wyatt gave her everything she wanted, everything she demanded of him.

When Teddie came beneath him, her body tensing, her head thrown back, her walls clenching around his cock, drawing him in deeper, it pushed him right over the edge. He let go with a groan that echoed off the bedroom walls, and everything went white.

The rain still fell outside, quieter, softer than earlier. Wyatt pressed his forehead to hers and kissed the tip of her nose. He rolled to his back, keeping her close, their limbs still tangled together, his hand gently caressing her back.

Teddie sighed and rested her head on his chest.

"That was wild," she whispered.

Wyatt chuckled. "You bring the animal out of me."

"I didn't expect that. I was just going to yell at you, then make you a cup of coffee." She giggled and kissed his chest. "This was better."

Wyatt hugged her and closed his eyes. "Much better."

Chapter 14
Teddie

Teddie grabbed a cup of coffee from the kitchen, hoping to see her mother and her sister before she went to work. They weren't anywhere around, so she took her mug and went to the guesthouse. She slipped in as quietly as possible, praying she wouldn't see her father. Fortunately, he wasn't around either.

Two hours later, she still hadn't seen or even heard anyone, but she'd gotten caught up on paperwork, done payroll, and spoken to the bank, only to find out she wasn't going to be able to make her father a counteroffer unless she found someone to co-sign for her loan.

Wyatt's offer to help hung over her head, but she couldn't bring herself to ask him to do something so phenomenally huge and life-changing. The prospect of marriage was crazy enough, without throwing in a multi-million dollar debt to start off their lives together.

She needed some air, so she pushed herself away from her desk and went outside. She considered going to the barn to see Wyatt, but she went to her mother's shop instead. Being around Maggie always made her feel better.

Teddie walked through the cherry orchard, admiring the trees stripped bare after the cherry harvest. She tapped twice on the shop's kitchen door, pushed it open, and peered around the edge. The familiar scent of sugar and fruit surrounded her.

"Hey, Mom."

Maggie wiped the flour from her hands and smiled at her eldest daughter. "Hi, sweetie, what's up?"

"I came by to see what you're up to," Teddie replied. "How goes the pie making?"

Before Maggie could answer, Tessa came out of the refrigerator with a giant tub of cherries in her hands. "Hey, Ted, how's it going?"

"Tessa? What are you doing here?"

Her sister shrugged. "Mom is showing me the ropes."

"Really? You haven't baked since you were a kid," Teddie said. "I thought you didn't like it anymore?"

"I don't know. I've been down here helping Mom for the last few days, and I kind of like it."

"She's got a knack for it, too," Maggie added with a smile. "Oh, by the way, I took a pie down to the barn for Wyatt yesterday. Did he bring it home?"

"Oh crap, I forgot to take one for him, didn't I?"

Maggie nodded. "But that's okay. I got to say hi and check on him." She opened the refrigerator, took out a pitcher, and filled two glasses. "Here, try my cherry lemonade and tell me what you think."

"Thanks." She sat down at a small table in the corner and sipped the lemonade. "This is good."

"Tessa, will you excuse us for a few minutes?" Maggie asked.

"You know what, I think I'll go to town and pick up some more sugar," Tessa said. She wiped her hands on a towel, tossed it on the counter, and then she was gone.

Maggie sat down across from Teddie. "Alright, what's wrong?"

She sighed. "What makes you think something is wrong?"

"I'm your mother," Maggie replied. "I can tell when something is bothering you."

"Did Dad tell you he agreed to let me make a counter-offer on the ranch?"

"Yes," Maggie said.

"Well, I can make the offer, but I won't have the money to back it up. The bank wants me to have a co-signer or find investors to front at least half of the money I need to purchase Cherry Ridge. I don't know how I'm supposed to find somebody to do that. Wyatt offered to help, but I don't feel right asking him to put up his entire life savings to help me buy this place. It's an enormous commitment."

"Do you think he's not ready for something like that?" Maggie asked.

"No," Teddie replied, dragging out the word. "I know he's ready to commit." She hesitated for a second, then blurted, "He wants to marry me."

She expected her mother to be more surprised or even emotional over the possibility of her daughter getting married, but she only smiled gently. "Sounds like he's okay with an enormous commitment to me."

"But how can I ask him to start our lives together with a huge debt hanging over our heads? That is so unfair to him."

Maggie got up and went back to the counter, where she returned to rolling out the dough for her pie crust. "Did you know I started the cherry shop in secret?" she asked.

"You did?"

Her mother smiled sheepishly. "Everett thought it was nothing more than a distraction." Maggie must have seen Teddie make a face, because she quickly said, "Oh, he never said that in so many words, but I heard it in his voice. He thought I needed a hobby, but I wasn't looking for something to pass the time. I wanted something that was mine. He indulged me by remodeling the staff kitchen and turning it into a little shop. I think he thought I'd get bored before too long."

Teddie laughed. "Daddy always said this was your hobby."

"I know." Maggie shook her head and laughed. "When I married your father, this ranch became my life, too. And even though I grew up on a ranch a lot like Cherry Ridge, I wasn't out chasing cows in the pasture. I was in the kitchen up to my elbows in flour and fruit in my apron pockets. Your grandmother taught me how to bake with the fruit we picked from the trees behind *our* house. The cherries were always my favorite. When we took over this place, those cherry trees were barely hanging on. I'm the one who brought them back to life."

"A lot of my memories from when I was little are of you in the cherry orchard taking care of your trees," Teddie murmured with a small smile. "And I remember helping you pit the cherries when I was little, my fingers stained red."

"Both you and Tessa used to help me." Maggie laughed. "Those are some of my favorite memories with you girls."

Teddie grinned. "Mine, too."

"Anyway, I started small, so small your father didn't even realize it was happening. I made pies for the farmer's market on Saturdays, then I added jams and jellies, cookies wrapped in twine and tucked in baskets. Next thing I knew, tourists stopped by on their way to Lakeside. Then it was locals who then became regulars. I started making more things, and before I knew it, the money was rolling in." Maggie paused and took a deep breath before she continued. "The shop does well, sweetie. Far better than anyone knows."

Teddie raised an eyebrow. "Oh?"

Maggie nodded. "Yes. But I've kept it to myself because I wanted to prove I could build something of my own, on my own, with no help. Just like you want to do with Cherry Ridge." She glanced up at her daughter, then returned her attention to the pie she was making. "I know what this place means to you, and how special it is."

Teddie swallowed, surprised at the swell of emotions rising in her.

"Please understand, I am not saying what I am about to say to undermine your father. But I have enough money saved from the shop to help you. I have enough to give you a real shot at buying Cherry Ridge. You don't have to lose the only home you've ever known because your father doesn't realize how much you love this place."

Struck speechless, Teddie stared at her mother for a long moment, the weight of everything pressing down on her. "You'd really do that? You'd give me the money?"

Maggie shrugged. "If you want to look at it that way. I see it as investing in your future."

Teddie jumped out of her seat, darted across the small kitchen, and threw herself at her mother. She hugged her while Maggie laughed and patted her arm with a flour-covered hand. When she stepped back, she had to wipe the tears from her eyes.

"Thank you, Mom. You don't know how much this means to me."

"No, I think I do," Maggie whispered, then she cleared her throat. "Let me get these pies in the oven, then we'll sit down and talk numbers. Pour yourself another glass of lemonade while you wait."

Teddie nodded and did as she was told. Her heart pounded in her chest, and her eyes kept leaking tears. She couldn't believe this was happening.

———

Teddie steeled her shoulders and knocked on her father's office door.

"Come in!"

She straightened her hair before she pushed open the door and stepped inside. "Hey, Dad, do you have a minute?"

Everett waved her in without looking away from the papers on his desk. Her father didn't have a computer on his desk; he liked to do things "the old-fashioned way."

Teddie eased into the chair across from him, clutching the folder with her counteroffer in her hands. She closed her eyes, willing the nervous rumble of her stomach to relax. It didn't help that her father took almost a full minute to put down the papers and look at her.

"What can I do for you, Theodora?"

She'd promised herself she wouldn't let her father get under her skin, no matter what he did or said. Using her full name was something he did to irritate her, especially when he was unhappy with her.

Teddie set the folder on her father's desk. "I brought you my counteroffer."

Everett opened the folder, glanced up at her, and then read every page. She kept still while he read; her father hated fidgeting. When he was done, he slowly closed the folder and folded his hands on top of it.

"This is impressive, Theodora," he said.

"Thank you," she mumbled.

He patted another folder beside hers. "I'm going to look over both offers, and I will let you know."

"That's it?" she asked.

Everett nodded. "Yes, that's it."

"Um, okay." Teddie got up and walked to the door. Her father cleared his throat, drawing her attention back to him.

"I'm serious, Teddie. This is superb work. I'm impressed with how much you put into this."

"Thanks, Daddy."

"I'll let you know by tomorrow," her father said.

As Teddie closed his door, her cheeks hurt from smiling. Her father didn't give praise often, so when he did, it meant a lot.

"Please let it be me," she whispered out loud.

"Let what be you?" an arrogant voice asked behind her.

She swung around to find Preston standing behind her with his sunglasses tucked in the front of his shirt and his baseball cap on backwards. His gum snapped repeatedly and annoyingly in his mouth.

"Preston! What are you doing here?"

"I came by to see your father." He narrowed his eyes. "He made it sound like you quit?" It wasn't a statement, but a question.

Teddie shook her head, her hair flying around her face. "No, I took a few days off. I needed to get my head on straight after everything that happened."

"Oh. Well, how's Wyatt?"

"On the mend," she replied. She smirked. "I think he's working today, if you want to say hello."

Preston made a face and shook his head. "I'm good." He pointed at the door behind her. "If you'll excuse me?"

Teddie stepped to the side and watched as Preston walked into her father's office without knocking. She rolled her eyes and walked away.

Now all she had to do was wait. It was going to be a long night.

Chapter 15
Wyatt

Wyatt flipped the pancake in the pan and checked the bacon in the cast iron pan, then he hit the button on the coffee pot. He had the plates on the table when Teddie walked through the kitchen door. Messy strands of her honey blonde hair framed her face, her eyes only half-open, wearing one of his thin T-shirts, barely skimming the bottom of her ass. She gave him a tired smile as she dropped into the chair at the kitchen table and poured herself a cup of coffee.

"Hi," he said, stopping to kiss the top of her head before he sat down across from her. "How'd you sleep?"

"I didn't," she mumbled. "I mean, I did, but not much. I'm so worried that Daddy will decide to sell the ranch to Preston instead of me. I cannot stop thinking about it."

Wyatt checked his watch. "Did he say what time he was going to let you know?"

Teddie shook her head. "No. Hopefully, he won't make me wait long."

As if on cue, her cell rang from the bedroom. She darted out of her chair so fast Wyatt had to grab it so it wouldn't fall over. He heard her speaking through the wall, but he couldn't make out what she was saying. He didn't like the look on her face when she came back to the kitchen.

"Uh oh, bad news?"

"It's not great news," she replied, tossing her phone on the table. "Daddy told Preston about my counteroffer, so late last night, Preston submitted a new offer. My father texted me about it last night, and honestly, I'm afraid I won't be able to compete with it."

"Did your father say that?" Wyatt asked.

"No. He hasn't gone over both proposals yet, but he wanted to let me know Preston submitted something new." She pushed her plate of food away and put her head on the table. "I'm screwed."

"Why do you think you can't compete with Preston's new offer?"

"Because it's Preston," Teddie muttered. "He probably offered an exorbitant amount of money that I can't match."

"Okay. Can you get a look at Preston's offer?"

Teddie's head popped up. "Hey, you know what? That's a good idea. I *can* get a look at it." She was on her feet again, headed for the bedroom.

A few minutes later, she emerged fully dressed. She kissed Wyatt on the head, mumbled, "See you later," and then she was gone.

"Bye," he muttered, eyeing her plate full of food. "Glad you enjoyed your breakfast."

Wyatt finished eating, took a shower, then he got in the truck and drove to the barn. When he walked into his office, Teddie was at his desk.

"Hi there," he said. "What are you doing at *my* desk?"

She held up a stack of papers and shook them. "I got Preston's offer off Daddy's desk and made a copy. I didn't want him to see me going over it, so I came down here." She grinned. "I hope that's okay?"

"Of course it is," he said. "Did you find anything weird?"

"Not yet."

"Let me know if you do. I'm gonna go feed the horses."

Teddie was still studiously looking over the offer when he finished feeding the horses, so he left her alone and made his way out to the pasture to check on the cattle. When he was done, he sent Luke and Ty to pick up hay while Hank and Nash cleaned the hay barn. After he'd finished all that, he returned to the barn. She was still at his desk, clutching the papers in one hand and gnawing on a pencil.

Wyatt leaned against the doorframe, watching her. "You're doing that thing where you chew on your pencil like you're punishing it."

She dropped the papers on the desk, along with her pencil. "I feel like punishing something. This updated offer *is* too good to be true, like I suspected. Supposedly, Preston got some new financial backers, making it possible for him to increase the purchase price. He also promised capital improvements to Cherry Ridge and that he will keep the current staff, including me *and* you."

"Really?" Wyatt stepped into the office, closed the door behind him, and crossed the room to the desk. He looked over her shoulder at the dog-eared papers with Teddie's notes scribbled in the margins.

"Yep. And there's more. He's going to lease the orchard to a nearby winery, but he promised to upgrade the equipment and housing on site, and he included a letter stating he and his investors plan on maintaining the ranch's legacy. But it's too good to be true. It's too... too *nice*. Preston isn't a generous person, and he doesn't care about legacies. Look what he did to his parents' ranch when his father passed away. He didn't give a shit about his legacy. The only thing he cares about is money."

"Let me see," Wyatt said.

She handed him the stack of papers, and he scanned it, brows furrowed.

"Where did these new investors come from?" Wyatt asked. "Do we know?"

Teddie shrugged. "According to the paperwork, it's a group of real estate investors out of Billings."

"I don't trust Preston," he mumbled. "You know what? Give me the names of the investors."

Teddie blinked. "What? Why?"

"I have a friend who works in agricultural financing in Missoula. He'll know if they're legitimate or not."

"I didn't even think about verifying the names," she whispered. "And you're willing to help me?"

"Of course I am. You're exhausted and stressed, Ted. Let me help you. Give me the names, and I'll call George."

Teddie jumped up and threw herself in Wyatt's arms, plastering his face with kisses. He chuckled as he hugged her.

"Thank you," she said.

"You're welcome." He kissed the tip of her nose. "I will not let Preston lie to the Colonel and get away with it. Or take this place away from you. Besides. I'd do anything for you."

"I don't deserve you."

"Yeah, you do." He hugged her close. "You deserve the world on a platter."

—

It took the rest of the day and into the evening for them to scour public records and for Wyatt to get the information on the investors from his friend. Once they had everything, it was far worse than they'd expected.

Wyatt grabbed one of the folding chairs leaning against the wall, put it next to his desk chair, and sat down. He spread the papers out on the desk.

"Alright, here's what George found out. These two investors, right here, these are names Preston used before in a land flipping scheme. This one is a shell company, and George can't find out any information about the owners. This guy is his cousin in Bozeman."

"Are you kidding?"

"I wish I were." Wyatt sighed. "And this one, he got himself blacklisted from a cattle co-op last year because he inflated the appraisal numbers."

"That asshole is selling a bunch of bullshit. It's a lie he's perpetrating to get my father's signature on paper. Once he does that, all bets are off." Teddie vaulted from her seat and paced the floor in front of the desk. "I need to talk to my father, convince him that selling to me is the best option."

"Well, go find him and talk to him," Wyatt said.

"I can't. When I went up to the house to get us food, I saw Tessa, and she said they took the RV to the other side of the lake to see how they like it. They won't be back until tomorrow."

"Then you've got time," he insisted. "Time to not only stop him from signing the agreement, but time to put together another proposal, a better one."

"A better one? How am I supposed to do that?"

Wyatt opened his desk drawer, took out the small velvet box, and set it on the desk. "Put together a proposal, including the money *your husband* is contributing, and explaining how the two of us are going to run Cherry Ridge together." He took Teddie's hands. "We can do this, you and me. You know we can. This ranch is your legacy, Ted, and together we'll make it the best ranch on Flathead Lake. This place will be *our* legacy, a place to raise our children, and someday pass on to our children." He grabbed the box and flicked it open. "So, Theodora Jean Calloway, will you marry me?"

Teddie nodded so hard her messy bun fell out of her hair. "Hell, yeah, I'll marry you!" She clambered into his lap, wrapped her arms around his neck, and kissed him, then she rested her forehead against his. "I can't wait to be your wife."

Wyatt took the ring out of the box and slipped it on her finger. "And I can't wait to be your husband. Now, let's get our offer put together, and then we'll go home and celebrate our engagement. Just you and me."

"That sounds amazing." She kissed him, her tongue sliding across his lips until he opened his mouth, her arms tightening around his neck, pulling him into her, her hips pressing into his.

Wyatt growled low in his throat. "If you don't stop that, we'll be celebrating right here on the desk."

Teddie giggled. "As fantastic as that sounds, let's get this offer done and go home. I want to spend some time with my fiancé."

Chapter 16

Teddie

*T*eddie parked her Jeep in front of the house. This was it, the moment of truth. Her father and mother had returned early this morning, and the Colonel had summoned her to his office.

Unfortunately, Preston had come, too. He'd parked his Mercedes in the circular drive.

She closed her eyes and took a deep breath. How in the hell was she supposed to keep her cool when Preston was here, the man who lied to get his hands on her family home? She exhaled and stepped out of the Jeep with her laptop bag in her hand. Her heart pounded as she walked through the orchard toward the guesthouse, clutching the strap of the bag like it was a security blanket.

Tessa popped out from behind a tree. "Hey, Teddie."

Teddie stumbled back a few steps and glared at her sister. "Jesus, Tess, you scared the crap out of me!"

Tessa grinned. "Sorry. I saw you pull into the driveway, and I wanted to talk to you."

"Well, hurry. I'm going to talk to Dad."

"About buying the ranch?" Tessa asked.

She nodded, one eyebrow raised. "Yeah. Why?"

"Can I talk to you about something?" Tessa said.

"Sure." Teddie dragged the word out, curious about what her sister wanted.

"If you get your hands on the ranch, I want in."

Teddie snorted. "What? You've never wanted anything to do with the ranch before. Why now?"

Tessa pushed a hand through her hair and sighed. "In case you hadn't noticed, I've been spending a lot of time with Mom. She's been, well, she's been kind of showing me the ropes and how she runs her shop."

"I noticed," Teddie said.

"I'd like to keep it open, if you buy Cherry Ridge. People in this town love Mom's pies and pastries, and it makes good money. That's the only thing I am asking. Give me control of the shop. I can make it bigger, like a bakery or a jam empire. Whatever. Anyway, I don't think it's too much to ask."

Teddie nodded. "You're right, it makes good money. And I don't think it's too much to ask. Besides, the person who really loves it is the person who should run it. Right?"

A small smile teased the corner of Tessa's lips. "Yep."

"But this entire conversation will be for nothing if Daddy doesn't take my offer for the ranch, so I need to go. I have to stop him from taking Preston's offer."

Teddie tried to walk past her sister, but Tessa grabbed her and hugged her so tight she couldn't breathe.

"Tess, gotta go," she mumbled.

"Yeah, sorry. Go in there and kick Preston's ass."

Teddie nodded, squeezed Tessa's shoulder, and hurried through the orchard to the guesthouse. When she stepped inside, she heard her father and Preston talking and laughing.

"Shit," she muttered under her breath, stepping up the pace.

She paused outside the door for a second, then she pushed it open.

"Hi," she said.

"Theodora," Everett said. "You're late."

Teddie glanced at the clock. "I'm two minutes late. I stopped to talk to Tessa."

He gave her a curt nod. "Well, have a seat."

She did as she was told, her knees bouncing as she sat down and put her bag on the floor beside the chair. She grabbed one folder from the bag and slid it across the desk. "You need to look at this."

Everett glanced at it, then back at her. "What is this? Your counteroffer." He shook his head. "I'm sorry, but it's too late. I've accepted Preston's offer."

Teddie stared at her father, willing him to listen to her. "Please, Daddy, look at what's in the folder."

With a hefty sigh, Everett flipped open the folder and read the first page. He glanced up at her and Preston, then he read it again.

"Are you sure about this?" he asked.

Teddie nodded. "Yes, sir." She cleared her throat. "Wyatt has a friend in ag financing in Missoula. He helped us figure this out."

"Us?"

"Wyatt helped me," she replied. "We stayed up half the night connecting the dots. He wants to protect Cherry Ridge as much as I do."

"Protect Cherry Ridge from what?" Preston interjected.

"From you," Everett said. He closed the folder and tossed it across the desk to Preston, who opened it and skimmed the first page.

"I don't know about any of this," Preston muttered. "This is obviously an attempt to disparage me so she can buy the ranch out from under me."

"Oh, really?" Everett leaned over the desk with a look she vividly recalled from her somewhat rebellious teenage years and, more recently, when he was angry with Tessa. Nobody lied to Colonel Calloway and got away with it. "Maybe I'll call Wyatt's friend myself?"

Preston's eyes widened as he looked between Everett and Teddie. "I... I don't think that's necessary. Besides, all of this is a moot point if Teddie doesn't have a counteroffer."

Everett turned back to her. "Alright, Theodora, do you have a counteroffer?"

"Yes." She removed another folder from her bag and handed it to her father.

He read through it, then he closed the folder. "This is more than your original offer. Do you have the money?"

"I have the money, Daddy," she said. "More than enough to buy Cherry Ridge. No investors, no strings. Just me and... and my husband."

Everett's brow furrowed, and he looked like someone pinched him. "Husband?"

Teddie held her left hand up and wiggled her fingers, showing him the diamond and sapphire ring on her finger. "Wyatt and I are getting married. We want to make Cherry Ridge our home, raise our children—your grandchildren—here."

"You're serious?" Everett said.

"I've never been more serious," she replied.

Everett stared at the top of his desk as he spoke. "I never wanted my children to feel obligated to run Cherry Ridge. My father didn't give me a choice; this place was mine whether or not I wanted it. I swore I wouldn't do that to you and Tessa. When I decided to sell the ranch, I thought I was setting you free."

"I'm not shackled to this place," Teddie explained. "I love Cherry Ridge. It's my home. I want to keep it that way."

"This is super sweet and all, but I have places to be," Preston interrupted. "Mr. Calloway, are you accepting my offer or not?"

She'd forgotten he was still sitting beside her. She folded her hands in her lap and waited for her father's answer.

Everett placed his hands flat on top of his desk. "I'm accepting Teddie's offer." He held up his hand before Preston could speak. "For a variety of reasons."

Preston opened his mouth to protest, but Everett pointed at the door. "Get out of my office. Now."

Everett waited until Preston had stormed out, then he opened the bottom drawer of his desk and pulled out a sheaf of papers. He dropped them on the desk.

"This is the contract to purchase Cherry Ridge," her father said. "I'm throwing it away."

"You're, you're … what?" she stammered.

"I'm not selling you the ranch, Theodora."

"I don't understand," she protested. "I have the money. I told you I want it—"

"I'm giving it to you," Everett interjected. "As a wedding gift."

Teddie swallowed and fresh tears welled in her eyes. "I don't understand. I thought you wanted me to buy it."

Everett shook his head. "I wanted to know in here," he said, tapping the center of his chest, "that you really wanted this place. I told you, I don't want to burden my children with something they don't want. You proved to me you want Cherry Ridge, so it's yours."

"Just like that?" Teddie asked.

Her father laughed. "Just like that." He tapped his fingers on the desk. "I'm sorry I put you through that, but for years I thought you were only here because I asked you to come home after college and help. I should have known how much this place meant to you. I'm sorry I didn't."

Teddie smiled. "It's okay, Daddy. I understand. I guess."

Everett blinked, then a smile spread across his face. "I'll call my lawyer and have him draw up the paperwork to transfer the ranch to you. It will only take a day or two."

"Okay," she whispered, smiling.

"Why don't you tell Wyatt the good news?"

"Yeah, I will." She was halfway to the door when she turned around, went around the desk, and hugged her father. "Thank you, Daddy. Thank you so much."

"You're welcome," Everett whispered.

Chapter 17
Teddie

10 Months Later

It was Teddie's favorite time of year at Cherry Ridge, when the rows of cherry trees were in full bloom, their soft pink petals fluttering in the light breeze. That's why she chose mid-May for the most important day of her life, more important than any other day ever.

Her wedding day.

She'd decided to have her wedding right here on the ranch she'd fought so hard for, beneath the trees she climbed as a kid, the trees that gave Cherry Ridge its name. There was no better place to marry the man she loved than the place she called home.

Teddie adjusted the headband holding the veil in place on top of her head and fixed the curl that kept flipping the wrong direction and falling over her eye. Then she checked to make sure she wasn't standing on the edge of her dress.

She squinted as she peered down the row of trees. Folding chairs formed two neat rows on either side of an aisle strewn with cherry blossom petals. Coarse twine tied wildflowers to each chair back, matching her bouquet. Maggie insisted on helping with the decorations, and now the ranch looked like a spread in some country bridal magazine, only better, because it was her ranch and her mother who had decorated it.

Tessa stood beside her in a pale pink dress, holding both of their bouquets. She poked Teddie in the arm. "Are you okay?"

She nodded. "I'm a little nervous."

"Well, don't faint or something while you're walking down the aisle," her sister said. "I don't think I can catch you in front of a hundred people. But holy hell, that would be a crazy photo to have in your wedding album."

Teddie giggled. "First, it's more like thirty people, counting the photographer and the caterer, and half of them are people who saw me face plant in cow shit last week. I think I'm good."

Tessa smirked. "That's true. Can't top that."

The music started, a soft guitar solo, courtesy of Hank, who could play anything by ear. Tessa handed Teddie her bouquet, kissed her on the cheek, and started down the aisle.

Everett stood next to her in his dress uniform, pride and something that looked suspiciously like emotion shining in his eyes. He held out his arm, and she took it.

Teddie kept her eyes on Wyatt as they walked through the trees. He waited at the end of the aisle in front of the two tallest cherry trees in the orchard on a small, raised platform. He wore a long-sleeved white button-down shirt, a green vest, his favorite Stetson, and the biggest smile she'd ever seen on his face.

She made it to the front without tripping, taking Wyatt's hand as soon as she was close enough.

He grinned at her and whispered, "You're awful pretty when you're not yelling at me about the irrigation schedule."

"If you'd do it like I asked, I wouldn't have to yell," she replied.

Luke—who'd gotten himself ordained so he could be their officiant—cleared his throat. Wyatt touched the brim of his hat with a smile.

"Ready when you are," he said.

Luke welcomed everyone and said a few brief words. He was charming and funny, just like Teddie knew he'd be.

"At this time, Teddie and Wyatt will exchange vows they have written themselves."

Tessa handed Teddie the ring she'd picked out for Wyatt. She smiled at him, took a deep breath, and clasped his left hand in hers.

"I love you, Wyatt Dawson. It didn't happen overnight, or like a bolt of lightning out of the sky, but gradually over time as I realized all the things that make you who you are. Like when you fixed the tractor without me asking, or stayed out in the pasture all night to help the cows give birth, or drove to Kalispell to get that flour my mom likes to use for her bread. You challenge me to be a better person and you don't take any crap from me. You stood by my side when things got tough and when I needed you, you were there. And somehow, through everything, I was lucky enough to find the man I love. I promise to fight for you no matter what. And if I need to fight with you, I'll do it, but only if you're being hardheaded. I'll laugh with you when the cows break the fence or cry with you when we have to put down our favorite horse. I promise not to micromanage your hay stacking if you promise to keep pretending you don't know where I hide my secret stash of chocolate in your office. And I promise to love you for the rest of our wild, crazy, messy lives if you promise to love me, too."

Wyatt laughed. "I promise."

Teddie slipped the ring on Wyatt's finger.

Luke chuckled. "Wyatt, your turn."

He cleared his throat, took Teddie's ring from his best man, Jesse, and squeezed Teddie's hand.

"I've been in love with you since the day you yelled at me to get my ass off your porch if I didn't plan on listening to what you had to say. And I knew I wanted to marry when you refused to give up the home you love. You are nothing but heart, Theodora Jean. I love that you don't back down, you don't give up, and you don't let anyone walk all over you—not even me. I will never try to tame you. I will keep your secrets, protect your dreams, and when the world gets too loud, I'll be your quiet place to hide. I promise to leave at least half of the last cinnamon roll for you and to always make sure you have a full cup of coffee. You are my best friend and the love of my life. I swear I will spend every day making sure you know how much you mean to me, even when you're yelling at me from the other side of the pasture."

Wyatt slipped the solid gold band onto her finger with hands still calloused from mending fences the day before.

When they kissed, it was a sweet, lingering kiss, even though the whole orchard was watching. They didn't give a damn.

Everyone clapped and shouted as they walked down the aisle past their friends and family. Someone whistled as Maggie dabbed the corners of her eyes. Everett's nod of approval meant more than anything he could have said.

"We did it," Teddie said with a smile.

"Yeah, we did." He kissed her forehead. "Now, let's go have a party."

—

The sun dipped behind the hills, leaving a gold haze over the ranch. The wedding crowd had thinned to the family, the McBrides, and the ranch hands. They'd gathered around the bonfire across from the barn, sipping drinks from small Mason jars. The flames crackled and popped, sending sparks into the clear night sky.

Teddie kicked off her shoes and padded across the grass, the hem of her dress gathered in one hand and a whiskey lemonade in the other. Wyatt stood by the fire, his vest long since taken off and his shirt sleeves rolled up to his elbows. He downed a glass of whiskey in two swallows. When he saw her, he held out his hand.

"Come dance with me, Mrs. Dawson."

She stepped into his arms without hesitation as a soft, slow tune played from the speakers hung on the outside of the barn. They moved together like they were one, her head on his shoulder, his hand resting lightly on the middle of her back.

Teddie looked around at the people she loved. Tessa and Luke were attempting to roast marshmallows over the fire, arguing about whether black or barely toasted brown tasted better. Her parents sat on a quilt by the fire with their legs stretched out, discussing their upcoming trip to Yellowstone in their new RV. Jesse and Claire danced a few feet from them while the other ranch hands sat around the fire talking.

"Ten bucks says you'll be out here tomorrow morning at six a.m., making a list of everything that needs to be done for cherry picking and worrying about the rain affecting hay season," Wyatt said. "And you'll probably still be in your dress."

Teddie laughed. "Twenty bucks says you'll be right next to me with coffee in your hand, taking notes."

They both took their responsibilities at the ranch seriously. There was never a day off, especially at this time of year. When they'd decided to get married in May, it was with the understanding that they'd postpone their honeymoon until later in the year. Teddie had joked they could wait until there was nothing to do, but then they'd never be able to go.

"Are you ready for this?" Wyatt asked.

"Yes. I've been ready for this my whole life. I'm right where I am meant to be with the person I'm supposed to be with. Together, we'll make this ranch greater than anyone imagined. Tessa has big plans for the cherry shop, and we've got the world on a platter. We can do anything we want."

"Anything?" Wyatt chuckled. "What are you thinking?"

Teddie pointed at the pasture in front of them. "What do you think of building a pen right there?"

"A pen for what?"

"Baby goats."

Wyatt shook his head. "Baby goats? Are you serious?"

Teddie nodded. "Yep. I *love* baby goats. They're adorable."

"Well, I guess we'll have to discuss that, won't we?" He wrapped his arms around her. "Maybe next spring. Unless we're busy with some other kind of baby."

She laughed, her face pressed against his chest. The world was hers. Whether it was baby goats or baby humans, she knew she could handle anything that came her way, as long as she had Wyatt by her side.

Want to get all the latest info about Mimi Francis and her upcoming projects and events? Subscribe to her newsletter on mimifrancis.com for exclusive news, stories, and updates.

Book Club Questions:

1. The setting of Cherry Ridge Ranch plays a huge role in the story. How does the landscape—especially the cherry orchard—add to the mood, symbolism, or emotional depth of the story?

2. Teddie's sister Tessa chooses to stay on the ranch and run the cherry shop. In what ways does her arc mirror or contrast with Teddie's? What do you think of their relationship?

3. Let's talk chemistry and heat. How did the chemistry between Teddie and Wyatt evolve? Were there particular moments that stood out as a turning point in their relationship for you?

4. Teddie wanting to stay at Cherry Ridge isn't just about the land—it's about her family legacy. How does the ranch symbolize more than just a physical place for her? What does "home" mean in the context of this story?

5. Family plays a complicated role in the story: from Everett's pride to Maggie's quiet support. How do each of the family members influence Teddie, and which relationships are the most emotionally impactful?

Author Bio

Mimi Francis is a sassy romance writer known for her steamy tales of passion that leave readers breathless. When she's not crafting the perfect happily-ever-after, you can find her sipping margaritas and binge-watching Marvel movies or the TV show Supernatural. But her true loves (after her husband, of course) are her four Shih Tzus who keep her company as she spins stories that will make your heart race and your toes curl. Get ready to fall in love with her characters and the worlds she creates.

Discover more at
4HorsemenPublications.com

10% off using HORSEMEN10

www.ingramcontent.com/pod-product-compliance
Lightning Source LLC
Chambersburg PA
CBHW030005010826

48973CB00009B/2666